VIENNAS AND VENDETTAS

CUP OF JO BOOK 10

KELLY HASHWAY

To Ayla with love

CHAPTER ONE

The morning at Cup of Jo couldn't be going smoother, and oddly enough, Jamar and Robin aren't here. I finally broke down and hired a third employee. I felt terrible for always overworking Jamar and Robin, even though they never complain. But seeing as how often my ex, Detective Quentin Perry, seems to rope me into helping him solve his cases with the Bennett Falls Police Department, I can't keep leaving my only two employees, who happen to be my friends as well, to run this place. Cup of Jo is my baby. My coffee shop. The best part might be Cam's Kitchen, the bakery portion run by my handsome fiancé, Camden Turner. Cam and I have known each other all our lives, and now we're business partners. If you ask my younger sister, Mo, she'll tell you Cam and I should be getting ready to walk down the aisle any day now, but we're taking our engagement slow—much to Mo's disappointment—and we plan to get married in a small ceremony right here at Cup of Jo—also to Mo's disappointment. I might be two years older than she is, but she thinks she should be in charge of my wedding anyway.

"Tables are all cleared, the counter is wiped down, and I'm getting ready to see who needs refills," Tyler Quinn, my new hire, says as he walks around the counter to where I'm making a Vienna for Mickey Baldwin, one of my regulars. It's his second Vienna of the morning, but he's sort of addicted to the special of the day.

"Tyler, slow down. You really don't have to wait on the tables. Everyone knows to come to the counter to order," I say. I appreciate his enthusiasm, and he's really a great worker, but I also don't want him to burn out his second week working here. Last week, Jamar and Robin trained him. This week, Jamar and Robin are finally getting days off while Tyler helps Cam and me here.

"Right. Sorry." He holds up both hands in apology.

I place my hand on his shoulder. "There's no need to apologize. You're doing great. Really. I couldn't be happier we hired you. But remember you get breaks, and you don't have to run around constantly."

He bobs his head. "Right. Got it. I just really want this to work out. Jamar and Robin speak so highly of you and Mr. Turner."

"Cam," I say, reminding him yet again that he doesn't have to call us Mr. and Ms.

"Right. Cam." That's another one of his quirks.

Every time I say something, his first response is "Right."
I'm hoping he gets comfortable here soon.

Cam comes out of the kitchen. "I need a taste tester,"
he says, looping one arm around me and kissing my
cheek. "You game, Jo?"

"Of course, but maybe Tyler can help, too," I say.

"Sure. Whatever you need." Tyler's like the over-
achiever in class who is always seeking the teacher's
approval. It's strange to me because the only employees
I've ever had are friends of mine. Sure, I met Robin
through Jamar, but she quickly became part of our group
of friends.

"Did I hear you say something about taste testing?"
Mo asks, walking up to the counter.

"Wow, you have good hearing," Cam says.

"Only when it comes to hearing things she wants to
hear," I say. "Maura Coffee has selective hearing."

"That's what happens when you have an older sister
who likes to remind you she has more life experience
than you do." Mo rolls her eyes, but her gaze meets the
specials board, she pauses. "What's a Vienna?"

"You'll like it. It's espresso, whipped cream, and
cocoa."

"Sounds great, and I'm sure it will go well with whatever it is Cam wants me to taste test."

"Is Wes meeting you here?" Cam asks her. Wes is
Mo's boyfriends, who happens to work across the street
with Mo at the advertising firm. They're both social

media whizzes. They've come in handy more than once when I have to help Quentin solve his cases.

"No, I can't stay either. We just needed mid-morning pick-me-ups." She holds out her hands. "Hence, I'm here. What are we taste testing anyway?"

"Banana hazelnut crumb cake," Cam says.

"Oh, that's going to be divine with Viennas," I say.

"I'll box two pieces to go and bring out two for you and Tyler," Cam says.

"I'll make the Viennas," Tyler says.

"How's it going with him?" Mo asks after Tyler rushes to make our drinks.

"He's pretty amazing. He's a total workaholic, though, and I'm worried he's going to burn himself out."

"He's only twenty-four, right? He's got plenty of energy." Mo is four years older than Tyler, but the way she says it, you'd think she had at least ten years on him.

Cam returns with Mo's to-go box. "Let me know what you guys think. I drizzled some dark chocolate over the top, figuring it would go well with the cocoa in the Viennas."

Mo takes the box, practically salivating. "You really are a good man, Camden Turner." Mo had a huge crush on Cam when we were growing up, but Cam always saw her as a younger sister.

He blushes and wraps an arm around me again. "Tell Wes we said hi."

Mo raises the box in the air. "Will do, and thanks for these."

"Here you go, Ms. Coffee," Tyler says, handing Mo a drink caddy with two Viennas."

"Just Mo," she tells him.

"Right. Mo." Tyler dips his head.

Mo smirks before walking out.

"Oh, I delivered the Vienna you made to Mr. Baldwin's table," Tyler tells me.

"Thank you, Tyler, but you are spoiling our customers."

"Oh, well, I know they love Jamar because he's so entertaining, and Robin is great with the customers, too. I just want people to like me. I didn't grow up here, and you know everyone in town loves their own."

He's not wrong. Bennett Falls is a small town, and everyone knows everyone else. At least if they grew up here. Some people aren't as quick to allow outsiders into our mix.

"You're young, Tyler. You have plenty of growing up left to do, and as far as I'm concerned, Bennett Falls is lucky to have you."

He smiles, and I hand him a piece of Cam's banana hazelnut crumb cake. "Let's sit down," I say.

"Let me grab our Viennas. I made one for you as well, Mr. Tur—Cam," Tyler says.

"Thank you, Tyler."

Cam and I find an open table and sit down.

"He's pretty great," Cam says.

"He is. I think he's going to work out just fine."

"But you want him to relax." Cam has always been good at reading my thoughts and emotions.

"With Jamar and Robin, it's like working with friends. With Tyler, I feel like his boss."

"Give him time. He's only been here for one week. I'm sure he'll relax soon enough."

Tyler walks over to us with three Viennas. "Here we go." He places them on the table, and then looks around the café. "Do you want me to check on the customers before I sit down?"

Everyone is seated with the food and drinks. Cup of Jo is a local hangout, and since all the kids are in school and most people are at work, the customers here on Monday mornings are my regular retirees, work-from-home patrons, or in Mickey Baldwin's case, nightshift workers having some snacks and socialization before calling it a day.

"Tyler, everyone is fine. Sit," I say.

He does, but he makes sure he is facing the majority of the customers in case anyone goes up to the counter to place an order.

Cam hands us each a fork. "Dig in."

I take a bite and immediately moan. "Cam, this is incredible."

Tyler tries his and nods. "This might be better than the Cups of Heaven."

Cups of Heaven are Cam's mousse creations in edible chocolate coffee cups. They're adorable and delicious.

"You think so?" Cam asks.

"Yes, and I hope that's okay for me to say. I'm not criticizing your Cups of Heaven at all. They're really good. Better than good, actually."

"Tyler, I know what you meant. It's fine," Cam says. "And food is subjective. One person's favorite is another person's least favorite. It comes with the territory."

"But everything you make is really delicious," Tyler says. "All of it. Seriously."

"Thank you." Cam turns to me. "So I should add this to my usual menu of baked goods?"

"Definitely." My phone rings in my pocket. "I'm guessing that's Mo to tell you exactly that." I answer the call, seeing her picture on the screen.

"You need to tell Cam to make this a permanent baked good," Mo says. No greeting or anything.

"We were just discussing that."

"It's seriously awesome, man," Wes says into the phone.

"Thanks. I'm glad you guys like it."

"Can you bring more to dinner tonight?" Mo asks.

"If there's any left," I say. "I'm not sure this will last long once word gets out."

"Make extra," Mo says. "What's for dinner anyway?"

"I think you meant to say, 'Jo, is it okay if we come for dinner tonight?'"

"Yeah, yeah. When do you ever say no?"

"Point taken. I'm making manicotti, salad, and garlic bread."

7

"Yum. We'll bring wine. See you then."

"Thanks for the crumb cake," Wes says before Mo ends the call.

"Is Jamar coming, too?" Cam asks.

"I'm not sure. He might have a date with Summer tonight."

"I should get back to work," Tyler says, finishing his crumb cake. "Thank you for this. I'm happy to pay for it."

"No way," I say. "You are welcome to free coffee and baked goods. Consider it part of your pay."

Tyler holds up his hands. "I couldn't do that."

"We do the same thing for Jamar and Robin," I say. "It's not up for debate."

"It's not worth your effort to try to argue with her," Cam says. "You won't win."

"You guys really are amazing bosses. I've never been treated this well on any job I've had. I don't even know what to say."

"Say you're just as happy to be here as we are to have you here." I smile at him before sipping my Vienna.

"I'm insanely happy to be working here."

"Good," I say.

He clears our empty plates before walking back to the counter to help customers.

"He's a keeper," Mrs. Marlow, my favorite seventy-year-old regular customer says, joining us at our table. Considering she's very loyal to lifetime residents of Bennett Falls, her endorsement of Tyler says a lot.

"We think so, too," I tell her.

Mrs. Marlow raises her eyes. "Don't look now, Jo, but that no-good ex of yours just walked in."

Quentin is one of Mrs. Marlow's least favorite people. When he cheated on me with my best friend, Samantha Shaw, who is now Mrs. Quentin Perry, the whole town sided with me in the breakup. Quentin still gets grief from it even though he's happily married and I'm happily engaged. And I'll admit that while I do help him solve cases with the BFPD, I like to remind him of his past indiscretions whenever possible. I think it's big of me to be civil to him and Samantha after they betrayed me, but as much as I can move past what happened, I'll never forget how much the two of them hurt me.

"Want me to tell him to get lost?" Mrs. Marlow asks.

Quentin and Samantha recently had their baby extremely prematurely. The poor boy couldn't go home from the hospital because he was fighting for his life. The situation sort of made me put my feelings aside because I can't even imagine what Quentin and Samantha are feeling.

"No, Mrs. Marlow. Quentin is going through a lot right now. I think it's best if we all cut him a little slack. At least until his son is able to come home from the hospital."

She considers it for a moment. "Okay, I suppose you're right. But after that..." She lets the rest of her sentence hang, and I wonder what she has planned for that time. I'm too scared to ask. The woman might be in her seventies, but you do not mess with her. I've seen her hit a man over the head with a coffee mug before.

Quentin approaches our table. "Jo, Cam, Mrs. Marlow." His tone is all business, and I know I'm not going to like where this conversation is going.

"Detective." Mrs. Marlow pats my hand on the table as she stands up. "You let me know if you need me, Jo. I'll be right over there. Watching." She glares at Quentin in warning. "Good day, Detective."

He dips his head, confusion all over his face. "How is it that she can make a simple greeting sound like a threat?"

"Because it was one. Don't worry about her, though. What's going on, Quentin?" I finish my Vienna.

"I hate to do this to you guys, especially on a Monday morning, but I don't have any other choice."

"Do what exactly?" Cam is glaring at Quentin now. He hates the man and only puts up with him for my sake. I can't blame Cam for not liking Quentin. Quentin has accused both Cam and me of murder before.

Quentin turns to look at Tyler. "That's your new employee, right? Tyler Quinn?"

"Yeah," I say. "Why?"

Quentin sighs. "Tyler's roommate was discovered murdered this morning."

"That's awful," I say.

"Yeah, well, it gets worse. The roommate's girlfriend found him dead on the living room floor."

My stomach drops because I know why Quentin is

here. "Did you even question the girlfriend before you came here to interrogate our newest employee?"

"She says they were supposed to meet for breakfast, and he didn't show, so she went to the apartment."

I scoff. "And that's it. You're here to haul Tyler down to the station because that's the easy answer for you."

"What do you expect me to do, Jo? His prints are all over the crime scene."

"Of course, they are! Tyler lives in that apartment. I'm sure he's touched just about everything inside it."

Mrs. Marlow stands up at my outburst. I hold up a hand to stop her from coming over here and introducing Quentin's head to her coffee mug.

"I'm only doing my job, Jo. I don't have to be talking to you right now, but I wanted to give you and Cam a heads-up before I take your employee out of here. You'll probably want to call Jamar to come in and cover Tyler's shift."

More like I'm going to have to call Jamar and Robin in to cover for Cam and me so we can make sure Quentin doesn't put Tyler in handcuffs without a lick of evidence against him.

"Would you be personally escorting him to the police station if he didn't work for us?" Cam asks, his face red with anger, which is typical when Quentin is around.

"This has nothing to do with either of you. I'm trying to solve a case."

"But coming here to accuse our newest employee and giving me a heads-up as you claim is also a great way to rope me into helping you solve the murder. Don't think I didn't notice that."

"I'm not looking for your help, Jo. I hate to break it to you, but Tyler is the guilty party, and I'm going to prove it."

"We'll see about that," I say.

Quentin turns on his heel and marches over to Tyler. He says something and then gestures to Cam and me. Poor Tyler. I can imagine what he's thinking right now. I stand up and walk over to them.

"Tyler, Cam and I will meet you at the station as soon as we get Jamar and Robin to cover for us here." I turn back to the table to see Cam is already on the phone. I'm sure he's calling Jamar.

"I don't know what's going on," Tyler says.

"I know. It will be okay. Go with Detective Perry, but wait until I'm there before you say anything."

"You're not his lawyer, Jo," Quentin says.

"If you'd rather he asks for one, go right ahead and try to stop me from being there. I don't think you'll be happy with the outcome."

Quentin clenches his jaw and shakes his head. Then he motions for Tyler to come with him.

"We'll be there soon," I tell Tyler.

As I watch them walk out, all I can think is that the universe is intent on forcing me to help Quentin solve his cases.

CHAPTER TWO

Jamar and Robin arrive at the same time even though they didn't carpool. Jamar is wearing a tight black T-shirt instead of his Cup of Jo shirt. "I wasn't sure if I had time to change," he says. "I hope this is okay."

"You're fine, Jamar. Thank you both for coming right in." I tell them what happened with Tyler and Quentin.

"I don't know Tyler well, but he seems way too nice to murder someone," Jamar says.

"I agree. My gut is telling me Quentin is jumping to the easiest conclusion yet again."

"I'll man the counter," Robin tells Jamar. "You take the floor." She turns to me. "We've got this. You guys go handle Quentin."

"Thank you both." I squeeze Robin's arm before following Cam out to his SUV. I'm pretty sure our cars can drive to the police station on their own at this point. I feel like we're always there.

I call Mo on the way, hoping she can get me some info on Tyler's roommate. Who he is, where he's from, etc.

"Hey, did Cam make more of that banana hazelnut crumb cake? I can't stop thinking about it," she says.

"Mo, I need you to find out who Tyler Quinn's roommate is."

"Tyler? As in the guy you and Cam recently hired?"

"Yes. Quentin just brought him down to the station for questioning. Apparently, Tyler's roommate was found dead in their apartment this morning."

"Oh. And you don't think Tyler killed him."

"You got it."

"All right. Let me see what I can find out. I'll call you back."

"Thanks, Mo."

We drive the rest of the way in silence. I'm not sure which one of us is angrier. Everything with Quentin always feels personal to us. He was the one who cheated on me, yet he seems out to get Cam and me on a regular basis. Maybe it's coincidence that Tyler started working at Cup of Jo last week and his roommate was murdered, but I'm sure Quentin came to get him in person instead of just calling him down to the station because it meant he'd run into me. He has a way of forcing me onto his cases. At first, he hated it when I butted my nose into his business like that, but now that he's sleep-deprived from spending all his free time at the hospital with his newborn son, he looks for reasons to involve me in his work.

Quentin is at his desk when we arrive, and Tyler isn't with him. "He's refusing to talk without you present," he says, not looking up from the file folder on his desk.

"Let's go then. We can get this over with, and you can find the real murderer."

Quentin finally looks up and meets my gaze. "You barely know this kid. Why are you so sure he didn't do this?"

Anyone who's spent ten minutes with Tyler would know he's not capable of murder. "He's like the sweetest kid ever."

"Or he's a good actor. How tough is it to pretend to be nice to your bosses?" Quentin asks.

"Probably not as tough as having an affair with your girlfriend's best friend," I say, not missing the opportunity to throw that in Quentin's face since he's insisting on acting like a moron.

He huffs as he stands up. "I'm not playing games here, Jo. If you aren't going to take this seriously, you can leave now."

I'm not about to leave Tyler in Quentin's hands. "Let's go talk to Tyler," I say.

Quentin walks around us, and we follow him to the interrogation room.

Tyler looks up at us the moment we enter. "I didn't do anything. Michael was fine when I left this morning."

"Then you saw him before work?" I ask, taking the seat across from Tyler. Cam stands behind me.

"Well, no. I heard him snoring, though. He snores really loud. Sometimes, it wakes me up even though we both sleep with our doors closed."

So he didn't see his roommate. He only heard him.

"What time did you leave the apartment this morning?" Quentin asks, sitting down and pulling out his pad and pen.

"I think it was a quarter after six."

"You start work that early in the morning?" Quentin looks at me to confirm.

"His shift begins at seven," I say.

Quentin cocks his head at Tyler. "It doesn't take forty-five minutes to get to Cup of Jo from your apartment. It's barely even fifteen minutes away."

"I know, but it was my first day without Jamar training me. I wanted to be early. I can't lose this job. Michael hasn't been making his portion of the rent payments, and I don't want to get kicked out. Jo and Cam are paying me more than my last job. I can't afford to get fired."

"No one gets fired for not being early to work," Quentin says. "Did you stop anywhere else on the way?"

"No. I went straight to work, and I helped Cam in the kitchen."

"That's true," Cam says. "He did help me. He washed all the bowls and utensils I was using to bake."

Quentin puts down his pen and laces his hands on

top of the notepad. "You made sure you had an alibi. That was smart."

"No, I—"

"Yeah, I think you and Michael had a fight over the rent he wasn't paying. Maybe you killed him by accident. Then you ran to Cup of Jo and threw yourself into your work so you'd have an alibi early in the morning before Michael would normally be up for the day. Does that sound about right to you?"

"No. That's not what happened." Tyler turns to me. "Jo, please, I swear. I woke up, and I went to work. That's it. I didn't see Michael at all. I didn't even eat breakfast before I left the apartment."

"I believe you, Tyler," I say.

Quentin sits back in his chair and crosses his arms. "Yeah, well unfortunately, I don't, and I'm the one you have to convince."

I glare at Quentin. "No, you're the one who has to convince a jury that Tyler is a murderer, and since he's not, you won't be able to."

Cam places a hand on my shoulder. As much as he'd love to punch Quentin in the face, Cam gets nervous when I threaten Quentin in any way.

Quentin lowers his arms and glares at me. "Jo, can we have a word outside?"

"No. I'm good here, thanks." I turn back to Tyler. "When was the last time you saw Michael?"

"Last night. He was on his way out. I didn't ask

where. I assumed he was seeing Tina. That's Michael's girlfriend."

"Yet she was the one who found Michael's body in the morning, so that doesn't exactly line up, now does it?" Quentin asks.

"Why?" I narrow my eyes at him. "They easily could have gone to dinner or a movie and made plans to have breakfast this morning. It makes perfect sense to me."

Quentin huffs. "Jo, I need to insist we speak outside for a moment."

I know Quentin. He's not going to let this go until he gets what he wants. He's like a toddler in that regard. I look at Cam, silently communicating that he should do his best to keep Tyler calm while I go see what Quentin wants. I stand up, and Cam rubs my arm as he takes my seat. I love that we can have conversations without saying anything at all.

I follow Quentin out of the interrogation room and to his desk. "What?"

"Look, I get that you think you know this kid, but he's my prime murder suspect. He had motive with the missing rent payments and opportunity because he lives in the same apartment."

"That's only two out of three, Detective." I stress the last word, letting him know I'm questioning his ability to do his job right now. "What about means?"

Quentin lets out a deep breath. "We don't have a murder weapon at this time."

"How did the victim die?"

"Michael Walberg suffered from blunt force trauma to the head. The medical examiner hasn't given us a possible murder weapon yet."

"I'm assuming you've searched the apartment."

"Of course. Like I said, the CSI team found Tyler's fingerprints all over the place."

I roll my eyes at the stupidity of that comment. Though I have to say it's a good way to cover up your fingerprints being on incriminating items if you live in the apartment where the murder occurred. It basically gives you a reason for having touched everything. I'll never say that to Quentin, though. He's ready to cuff Tyler as it is.

"Can I see the crime scene?" I ask, knowing the body will have been removed by now so there's no chance of having to see it.

"You want me to ask Chief Harvey to bring you on as a consultant?" he asks.

"No, I'm asking you to bring me to the crime scene. Whether or not you tell Chief Harvey is up to you." The chief doesn't exactly hire consultants; however, he has accepted my help and told me it was my duty to reveal any of my findings to the lead detective on the case. That's Quentin, so I highly doubt the chief will object to me getting involved. Do I think I'll get paid for my time and effort? I'm not holding my breath. Still, I can't sit back and leave Tyler's fate in the hands of Quentin Perry.

"If I do this—"

I hold up a hand to stop him. "Don't act like you'd be doing me a favor. We both know it's the other way around. Without me, you're going to arrest the wrong person and look like a fool in court. If that's the route you prefer to take..." I hold up both hands, gesturing "oh well."

Quentin shakes his head. "You know, I never come into Cup of Jo and try to tell you how to make coffee."

"Today's special is a Vienna. Do you even have the slightest clue what that is?" I ask.

He clears his throat. "All right. Here's what I'm going to do. I'll let Tyler go. For now." He pauses for dramatic effect. Or maybe I'm supposed to thank him for that small favor. I'm not sure. "Then we'll go to the crime scene. But I'm telling you we will be talking to Tyler again because I'm not leaving that apartment until I find something."

"Fine. Let's go." I stand up.

Quentin leads the way back to the interrogation room. "Mr. Quinn, you're free to go for now, but you can rest assure I will be in touch again soon, so don't plan to leave town."

Tyler stands up and looks at me. "I'm really free to go?"

"Cam and I will drive you back to Cup of Jo," I say.

"I thought you were coming with me to the crime scene," Quentin says.

"We'll meet you there after we drop off Tyler."

Quentin looks annoyed but doesn't say anything.

We walk out of the station and get in Cam's SUV.

"I'm so sorry about this," Tyler says. "You guys probably don't want me to work for you anymore, right?"

"Tyler, I can't say you're the best worker we've ever had because Jamar and Robin are fantastic as well, but we're not about to fire you over this. That wouldn't be fair at all."

"Should I get a lawyer? I'm not sure I could afford one."

"I don't think you need to worry about that just yet."

The rest of the ride back to Cup of Jo is quiet. I'm sure Tyler is scared to death right now. "Are you okay to work for the rest of the day?" I ask him once Cam parks.

"I'd prefer to. I don't want to go home since that's where Michael died, and if I don't keep busy, I'll stress out over all this."

"Okay, tell Jamar and Robin that one of them is free to go home. Let them decide," Cam says.

Tyler nods. "You two are really going to my place to look for clues? Do you do this sort of thing often?"

"More often than I like," I say.

"Well, thanks. I can't tell you how much I appreciate this. I wish there was something I could do to clear my own name." He opens the car door and steps out.

That gives me an idea. In cases like this, it can be little details that help find the guilty party. It's possible Tyler knows something important and doesn't even realize it. "Tyler, I'm making dinner at my place tonight. I'll text you the address. I think you should come."

"Really? You watched me get hauled into the police station because I'm suspected of murdering my room-mate, and you're inviting me to your place for dinner?"

I bob one shoulder. "Detective Perry is my ex. I sometimes feel responsible for the stupid things he does, so let me make it up to you by cooking you dinner."

"Can I bring anything?"

"A clear mind. I'm going to need to pick your brain about this case."

He nods, and the fear in his eyes seems to bore into me. "Thank you."

"I'll text you the address and time," I say.

He nods one more time before closing the door.

When we hired Tyler, I put his phone number and address in my contacts, so I pull up the address and click on the navigation. As Cam drives, I ask, "What happened when I went to talk to Quentin?"

"Tyler just told me how scared he was. He didn't understand why he's a suspect. I tried to tell him Quentin tends to find the easiest way out of his cases. Tyler's from a big city originally, and he's not used to small-town life yet. He said he sort of feels like an outsider here. He said coming to work for us was the best thing he could have done in more ways than one. It made our regulars accept him since we hired him, and now we're helping him with this case."

"He seems like a good guy. He's so polite and eager to please others. I can't imagine him beating his room-mate to death."

"Michael was beaten to death?" Cam turns to look at me briefly.

"Yeah, Quentin said they don't have a murder weapon yet, but cause of death was blunt force trauma to the head."

We arrive at Tyler's apartment. It's a house that appears to have been divided into four apartments. Each has its own outside entrance, which means there are two doors on the first level and stairs on each side of the house leading up to the front doors upstairs. It's an odd design. Quentin is standing in front of the door on the second level on the right side.

Cam parks, and we walk up to meet Quentin.

"I can't believe you trust that kid in your place of business when you're not there," Quentin says.

I trust Jamar and Robin completely, and I know Jamar will be the one to stay behind with Tyler today. I'm not worried in the least. Jamar is a former physical trainer. He's in incredible shape. Tyler probably couldn't hurt him if he tried, not that I think he would try. "Let's focus on finding clues at the crime scene, okay?"

"Right. You can butt into my work, but I can't inquire about yours." Quentin turns and opens the front door, which has yellow police tape across it.

"Glad we got that cleared up," I mumble as I follow Quentin under the police tape.

The front door opens right into the living room. There's blood on the beige carpeting a few feet from the door.

"It looks like Michael might have been answering the door," I say.

"His body wasn't facing the door. It was facing the opposite direction," Quentin says, sounding a little too happy to prove me wrong, but really, he solidified my point.

"Exactly. So he answered the door, let the killer inside, and then was hit over the head," I say.

"That means he knew his killer," Cam says.

Quentin puts one hand in the air. "Hold up. We don't know that at all. You're speculating."

"You're right. It's possible someone came to the door asking for something, and Michael turned back inside to get it. The killer could have followed him and attacked."

"Again, speculation."

"You're just angry because I've only stepped two feet inside the apartment, and I already have a better theory than you do."

"Until you can prove any of it, you've got exactly nothing." Quentin crosses his arms in front of his chest.

I want to argue, but he's right. We have nothing to prove Tyler didn't kill his roommate.

CHAPTER THREE

Cam and I walk through the rest of the apartment. The kitchen doesn't look like anyone uses it other than to get food from the refrigerator. I'm pretty sure the stove has never been turned on. The cabinets contain paper plates and plastic cups, so I'm doubting that Tyler and Michael even have dish soap in this place.

Tyler's room is neat. His bed is made, and all his clothing is hung in the closet. I can't help noticing the hangers look like the ones that came with the clothes. He must shop at stores that allow you to take the hangers when you purchase the clothing. There's no dresser or nightstand, only a bed. Tyler is definitely hurting for cash by the look of this place.

Michael's room is the complete opposite of Tyler's. The bed is unmade, and nothing is hung in the closet. There's a popup hamper in the corner, overflowing with heaps of clothing. Several pairs of sneakers litter the bottom of the closet. There's a card table with empty paper plates in one corner, and a small television sits on an old dresser across from the bed.

"Remind me to ask Tyler how he met Michael. They don't seem to have much in common."

Cam nods. "There's nothing in here that looks like it could be used as a weapon either. I'm thinking the killer might have brought it with him."

"That's possible and would explain the element of surprise." I walk back to the living room where Quentin is bending down to inspect the carpet where the blood spot is.

"Find anything?" he asks us.

"Not really. I mean, they appear to be polar opposites, but I'm not sure that matters in the grand scheme of things."

Quentin stands up. "I don't know. Being different means they probably had a lot to fight about." He rubs the back of his neck. "Did Tyler have anything with him when he showed up to work this morning?"

"You mean like a murder weapon?" I shake my head. Why does Quentin always think his cases should be that straightforward? "Sorry, but no."

"Did you search his car?" Cam asks.

"No, not yet. I'll need a search warrant for that."

I might not. Being that I'm Tyler's boss, and I'm trying to clear his name, he might allow me to look through his car. Of course, I'm sure Quentin would say I tampered with evidence if I beat him to the search. But what Quentin doesn't know won't hurt me.

"I'm thinking maybe Tyler left, like he said he did, but he forgot something, so he came back." Quentin looks around. "Maybe he forgot his keys. That would mean he'd knock and Michael would have to answer the door." Quentin moves toward the door and then takes a few steps into the living room, mimicking the path Michael could have taken. "Tyler could have hit him over the head without Michael ever being able to defend himself."

"Okay, but that means someone might have seen Tyler leave and go back for his keys. Did you question the neighbors?"

"They aren't home, so not yet."

"I'd like to talk to whoever lives in the apartment next to this one. They might have heard something," I say.

Quentin pulls out his notepad. "That's Gabrielle Santos. She's a twenty-six-year-old waitress at the Bennett Falls Diner."

"I could eat," Cam says.

"I heard they have great French toast. It's that Texas style toast that's really thick." I hold up two fingers spaced over an inch apart to demonstrate.

Quentin pulls his phone from his back pocket. "I need to check in with Sam, but I'll meet you two there."

Oh goodie. Lunch with Quentin.

The diner is packed since it's lunchtime, but we manage to get a table in the back. It's only a two-seater, so I'm not sure where Quentin plans to sit when he gets here. Gabrielle isn't our waitress. We have some guy named Steve serving us. We place our orders, both opting for the French toast and coffee. I know I'll be disappointed with the coffee, but I might be a little bit of a coffee snob since I run my own coffee shop.

Quentin shows up a few minutes later and flashes his badge at the hostess. She motions to our table.

"Was that really necessary?" I ask. "You knew we were getting a table."

He looks around for an empty chair, finding one at a nearby table. When the two women seated there tell him he can take the chair, he drags it over and sits between Cam and me. "I'm on official police business. This way, when I ask to speak to Gabrielle Santos, I won't have to deal with hearing how she's too busy to talk to me right now."

Steve returns with our coffees and takes Quentin's order. He gets a cheese burger deluxe and a chocolate milkshake, which earns him a look from me.

"What? Samantha's on a diet to lose the baby weight, so I can't eat like this at home. We have salad every night. I've already dropped ten pounds, which just makes her angry with me."

"So eating like a teenage boy and putting on weight is all in the name of saving your marriage?" I mock.

"Kind of, yeah." Quentin bobs a shoulder. "Have you located Gabrielle yet?"

"We only beat you by a few minutes. All we did was order."

Quentin looks around. There's a waitress serving the table next to ours, and he flags her down.

"Do you need me to get your server for you?" she asks as she approaches our table.

"No," Quentin says. "We need to speak with Gabrielle Santos. Do you know where she is?"

"Gabby is usually stationed on the other side of the dining room." She looks past us. "I don't see her. Maybe she's in the kitchen. I can go check for you."

Quentin holds up his badge. "I'd appreciate that."

The sight of the badge makes the waitress tense. "Is Gabby in trouble?"

"No," I say. "We're friends of her neighbor. He told us to ask for her if we came in for lunch." Quentin and his stupid superiority complex. I swear you'd think he'd figure out people are more likely to open up to me because I don't flash a badge in an attempt to intimidate them. The man can be really dense at times.

"I'll go see if I can find her." She hurries off toward the kitchen, and I have a feeling we won't see much of her again. I bet she'll try to avoid our table as much as possible.

"Would you ease up with the badge?" I say, reaching for my coffee and taking a sip. It's strong, and not in a good way. More like it's been sitting out for a while. Given that it's lunchtime, I'm willing to bet the pot is from breakfast. I put down the cup. "Gabrielle Santos didn't do anything, but if that waitress tells Gabrielle a cop is looking to talk to her, you're going to put her on the defensive before you even open your mouth. It's not a smart tactic."

"Don't tell me how to do my job, Jo. There's a reason your badge is invisible."

My invisible badge is something that started with me mocking Quentin when he first asked me to do impossible things like detain suspects. But it's become a joke since then. Quentin's not joking now, though.

"Maybe Cam and I should take our food to go if you're so sure you've got this case under control."

"Hey, would you two stop fighting? I think Gabrielle Santos is coming this way." Cam juts his head in the direction of the brunette woman walking toward us. She looks to be about Tyler's age. Maybe a few years older.

"Hi," she says. "Lilia said you wanted to speak with me."

"Yes, hi. I'm Jo, and this is Cam. We own Cup of Jo on Main Street."

"Oh yeah. I've been there. You have amazing baked goods." She leans down toward the table and whispers, "Don't tell my boss, but your desserts are so much better than ours here."

"Thank you," Cam says. "And I won't tell a soul."

She laughs. "Thanks. What can I do for you?"

"Well, your neighbor, Tyler Quinn, works for us."

"Oh, I didn't know Tyler got a job working at Cup of

Jo. We don't talk much. It's more like polite greetings in passing. You know how it is."

"Is it like that with Tyler's roommate, too?" I ask. I don't want to tell her Michael is dead. There's a good chance she doesn't know since she's been working all morning.

"That guy? No. I don't talk to him at all. He's…strange."

"How so?" I ask, and my gaze flits to Quentin, who is being oddly silent. Maybe he recognizes I'm getting Gabrielle to open up to us, and he's smart enough to keep his mouth shut so he doesn't ruin it.

"Well, he doesn't have a job. I think he might have for a little while, but then he was at the apartment all the time. I could hear his music through the walls. Tyler is quiet, but his roommate is loud. He has one of those voices, too. You know, the type that sounds like it's always on full volume."

"Did you hear him this morning?" I ask.

"Yeah, right before I left I heard him yelling at someone. I guess he was on the phone or something. I've heard him yell at the TV too, though, so don't quote me on that."

"Did you hear another voice?" Quentin asks, finally speaking up.

She shrugs. "I don't know. I was in a hurry. My alarm didn't go off, and I didn't want to be late for my shift here."

"Did you see Tyler leave this morning?" I ask.

Gabrielle's eyes narrow. "Why are you guys asking all these questions?"

I guess we can't keep Michael's murder a secret from her if we want her full cooperation. "Tyler's roommate, Michael Walberg, was found dead in the apartment this morning."

"Dead? What happened to him? Did he overdose?"

"Did he use drugs?" Quentin asks.

"I don't know." She holds up both hands. "I was just taking a guess. The guy seems shady, so I figured maybe he used drugs. For all I know, he deals them, too. That could be why he doesn't go to work. He could be making money from selling drugs. He's really dead?" She seems bothered by the fact that someone died in the apartment next to hers. It's always disconcerting when a death occurs close to home, so I understand that. I've had murders occur way too close to where I work.

"What time did you leave your apartment this morning?" Quentin asks her.

"Um, I was running a little late, but it couldn't have been after six thirty."

That would mean Michael was up shortly after Tyler left the apartment at six fifteen. Someone else could have shown up in that fifteen-minute window, and that someone might have been the murderer.

"Did you see any cars in front of the house when you left? You know, cars that don't belong to the other tenants?"

"Um, yeah, but I think the car belonged to someone

who's here a lot. I recognized it. It's a beat-up old sedan. It's like this rusty reddish orange color. It's hard to miss."

Quentin grabs his notepad and pen and jots down the description of the car. "But you didn't see anyone near the apartment next to yours, and you can't be sure if Michael was talking to someone inside the apartment?"

"Not really, no." Gabrielle's eyes widen. "Wait. Was he murdered? Did someone kill him? Do you think they were inside the apartment with him when I left?" Goose bumps pop up on her arms, and she rubs at them. She's really freaking out. "Should I be afraid to go home? I mean, I always lock my doors, but I live alone. Will I be safe there?"

I wish I could offer her some reassurance, but we don't know if the killer was targeting Michael Walberg specifically or not. We don't know much of anything. "Do you have a friend you could stay with for a few days?" I ask her.

She presses a hand to her mouth.

Quentin glares at me. "Miss Santos, there's no reason to think you're in danger," he tells her.

"No, but if you'd feel safer staying with a friend until this case is solved, then you should do that," I say. "For peace of mind."

She bobs her head. "You're a cop, right?" she asks Quentin.

He nods and pulls a card from his pocket. "If you remember anything else, call me."

"Can I go back to work now?" she asks.

"Yes, thank you for your help," I say.

She's shaking as she walks away.

"Way to scare her, Jo," Quentin says.

"She was already scared, Quentin. I was trying to help her find a solution so she wouldn't be living in fear until we find the killer."

Cam reaches for my hand, trying to get me to calm down before this turns out to be another full-blown fight with Quentin.

Steve returns with our food, but even though the French toast looks amazing, I've lost my appetite.

Mo and Wes show up for dinner at six. I told Tyler to be here at six thirty because I wanted to talk to Mo before Tyler gets here.

"It smells great in here," Wes says. "My lunch was a yogurt, so I'm famished."

"Sounds like you had a working lunch," I say, taking the two bottles of wine from him.

"It was my own fault. I'm struggling with this ad campaign. The client is picky, and it's messing with my head. I'm so afraid to disappoint them that I can't think creatively at all. I'm totally blocked."

"You'll figure it out," Mo says, grabbing wine glasses from the cabinet. "You need a drink to relax." She grabs a bottle from me and opens it. "I had a busy day, too, so I didn't have much time to look into Tyler's roommate for you. But the weird thing is I couldn't find any record of Tyler even having a roommate. So even if I did have more time to search, I don't think I would have found anything."

"His name must not have been on the lease," Cam says.

"That's right. The rental agreement is only in Tyler's name," Mo says, pouring a glass of wine and handing it to Wes.

"Maybe Tyler was subletting the second bedroom to Michael," I say. "We'll be able to ask him soon because I invited him to dinner."

Mo hands me a glass of wine. "Why did you do that?"

"Because I don't think he's a killer, and we need to figure out who is."

"How was working with Quentin today?" Wes asks. "Has he mellowed at all, or is he still on edge all the time?"

"You mean is he still acting like he has a stick up his—"

I hold up a hand to stop her. "Mo, we all know how you feel about the man."

"Yeah, and we all know you're way too forgiving." She rolls her eyes.

"I'm doing this to help Tyler, not Quentin."

While dinner is cooking, we sit down in the living room.

"How did you meet Tyler, anyway?" Mo asks.

"He applied for the job opening at Cup of Jo," I say, leaning back against Cam, who puts his arm around me so we can snuggle up on the couch like usual.

"Then how can you be so sure he's innocent?" Mo sips her wine, her brow furrowed. "You don't know anything about him. Where's he from?"

"He grew up in Philadelphia. He said he wanted to get away from the big city and all the crime." I scoff. "I guess that second part didn't work out so well for him."

"Does Quentin know where Tyler is from?" Wes asks. "He'd probably use it against him."

"I'm sure he does. But Tyler is so sweet and polite and responsible. Call me crazy, but I trust him."

"Crazy," Mo says with a smirk. "And now we're going to have dinner with him thanks to you."

"Um, hi," Tyler says from the open doorway. None of the residents of my apartment complex close their doors when they're home. That way the resident black cat, Midnight, can come and go as she pleases. We all take care of her as if she were our own.

I'm sure Tyler heard what Mo said, and I flash her a disapproving look as I stand up from the couch. "Come on in, Tyler."

"Are you sure? I understand if you changed your mind." He lowers his head.

"Not at all. Come in. I'll get you some wine." I wave him inside.

"Is he even old enough to drink?" Mo asks. She's in

the kitchen now, practically blocking Tyler's path into the apartment. Wes is at her side.

"Mo!" I can't believe she's being so rude.

Tyler pulls his hand from around his back, and Mo screams. Like actually screams. Before I know what's happening, Wes lunges at Tyler and tackles him to the ground.

CHAPTER FOUR

I grab Wes's arm and tug. Cam rushes around me and helps Tyler to his feet.

"Are you okay?" Cam asks him.

"What were you doing?" I ask Wes.

Wes looks horrified. "He has something behind his back, and Mo screamed, so I thought..." Wes stops talking, but I know he thought Mo saw some sort of weapon in Tyler's hand.

Tyler hands me a bouquet of flowers, which are squished from Wes tackling him. "I didn't want to come empty-handed, but it's clear I shouldn't have come at all."

"No, Tyler," I say. "Please stay. You didn't do anything wrong, and it was very sweet of you to bring me flowers."

Cam looks at me, and I'm not sure he feels the same way about another man bringing me flowers.

"My mom taught me you always bring flowers for the hostess when you're invited to dinner." Tyler lowers his gaze.

"Sorry for tackling you," Wes says. "I hope I didn't hurt you."

"My ego is the only thing that got bruised, but I guess I have to expect people to react this way to me since I'm a suspect in a murder."

"It's not your fault your roommate was murdered in your apartment," I say. "If anything, you're a victim, too."

"Jo's right," Cam says. "Please come in."

Tyler looks at me, and I nod. He takes a few tentative steps inside. "Nice place."

"Thank you," I say, grabbing a vase for the flowers and filling it with water. "And thank you for the flowers."

"So, Tyler, why isn't your roommate listed on your rental agreement?" Mo asks as if she's leading an investigation.

"Oh, well, I thought I was going to be able to handle the rent on my own, but after paying all the utilities on top of the rent, I realized I could use a roommate to split expenses with."

"But he didn't pay the rent directly to you?" Mo asks.

"I wasn't subletting. My landlord, Mr. Worthington, said Michael could pay him half the rent."

"Why wouldn't he put him on the rental agreement then?" Mo asks.

Tyler shrugs and puts his hand in his pockets. "I don't

know. You'd have to ask him, but maybe it just slipped his mind."

"How did your landlord react when Michael didn't pay his share of the rent?" Wes asks.

"He showed up a few times, trying to collect."

"Trying to?" I ask. "You mean Michael never paid?"

"He did a couple times. It would take Mr. Worthington showing up about six times before Michael would finally hand over the money, though."

"Did he pay in cash?" Cam asks.

"Yeah. Why?"

"Most people would write a check," Cam says.

"That's what I do, but I think Michael was trying to get Mr. Worthington off his back and thought cash might be the way to do it."

If this Mr. Worthington isn't on the up-and-up, he might have pocketed the cash and wrote off half the rent as a loss since there's no paper trail. He might be worth looking into.

The timer on the stove goes off, so I pull the manicotti out of the oven and stick the garlic bread in on broil. "Have a seat. We can start with salad while the garlic bread is cooking."

Cam carries the giant bowl of salad to the table for me and starts dishing it out. A few minutes later, all the food is on the table, and everyone is eating.

"Delicious as always, Jo," Wes says.

"Thank you."

"Food always tastes better when someone else makes it," Mo says. She's never liked cooking.

"Look out, Wes. If you stick with my sister, you're in for takeout for the rest of your life."

"We're not eating takeout now, are we?" Mo asks with a smirk.

"Oh, so you plan to mooch off me forever. Good to know." I shake my head.

"Do you guys do this a lot?" Tyler asks. "Have dinner together, I mean."

"Mo hates cooking, so she usually winds up here at dinnertime. Jamar comes here a lot, too. He lives right next door."

"Really? I could tell you two were close, but I didn't realize you were neighbors."

"How well do you know your neighbors?" I ask. "We spoke to Gabrielle Santos today at the diner."

"You went to the diner without me?" Mo whines. "Don't even tell me you got the Texas French toast. I won't speak to you for a week."

"I got the Texas French toast," I say without hesitation.

"You're dead to me, Jo Coffee. Dead."

Tyler laughs and looks at Cam. "Are they always like this?"

"For as long as I've known them, and we all grew up together."

"Wow. It must be nice. In my old neighborhood,

people came and went all the time. I didn't have a single friend that I grew up with for more than a year or two."

"That's sad," Mo says. "It must make it hard to form relationships with people now, too."

Is she trying to find out if there was tension between Tyler and his roommate?

Tyler looks down at his plate. "I'm the type who talks to everyone, but I'm always expecting people to walk out of my life with no notice." He bobs one shoulder. "It's just how it goes for me."

"Well, you won't find better friends than Jamar and Robin," I say, getting up to grab the garlic bread from the oven. "If you're looking to make friends, that is."

"I am. It's lonely living by yourself. Even with Michael, it was like I was alone. He didn't really interact much with me. He kept to himself."

"How did you meet him?" I finish putting the garlic bread into a basket and bring it to the table.

"I put up flyers advertising a room for rent. He called to ask about it. I didn't have anyone else inquire, so I said yes to Michael."

"Gabrielle said Michael had a job for a while but has been out of work recently," I say before taking a bite of manicotti.

Tyler nods. "He worked at a gas station for a little while. I don't know what happened, if he quit or got fired, but he was there for about three weeks."

"When we told Gabrielle that Michael was dead, her

first question was if he died of a drug overdose," Cam says. "Did Michael do drugs?"

"I don't know. He always had his bedroom door closed. I didn't smell weed or anything, but I guess he could have been using other stuff without me knowing."

"Did he have visitors a lot?" Mo asks. "You know, the kind that didn't stay long?"

Tyler cocks his head at her. "You think he was dealing drugs out of our apartment?" The cracking of his voice makes it clear he's horrified by that idea.

"Could have been," Mo says.

Tyler looks green, and he puts his fork down. "I think I should have looked into him more before I let him move in. There are so many Michael Walbergs online, though. The name was too common to really look into."

"It is tough to research people online when they have a common name," Mo says. She pulls out her phone, and I know she's typing in Michael Walberg. "Yeah, there's more than one in this state alone and multiple across the country."

"Will you be able to find out some info for us?" I ask her.

"I'll do my best." She pockets her phone. "After dessert that is."

I roll my eyes. Cam brought home a banana hazelnut crumb cake as per Mo's request. We finish dinner and then bring dessert to the living room with our coffee. Since I have banana hazelnut coffee, I brew a pot of that to compliment the crumb cake.

"Is this a typical evening for you guys?" Tyler asks.

Midnight chooses that moment to walk into the apartment with a loud meow to announce her arrival.

"Whoa! Someone's cat walked right in," Tyler says.

"Now it's a typical evening here," I say, scooping up Midnight. "Midnight, say hi to Tyler. Tyler, meet Midnight, the resident cat of this apartment complex. We all sort of take care of her."

"Hi, Midnight," Tyler says, scratching Midnight's head. "Are you looking for food?"

"She knows I always have tuna in my fridge for her," I say. "Here, do you want to hold her while I get her dinner ready?"

"I'd love to. I've always wanted a pet, but my mom was allergic, and now that I live on my own, I can't afford another mouth to feed." He takes Midnight, cradling her like a baby, which she seems to like judging by the purring that ensues.

"She likes you," I say, grabbing the tuna from the fridge and scooping some into Midnight's food bowl in my kitchen. I get her some fresh water as well, but she's so content in Tyler's arms at the moment that she couldn't care less about eating.

"You said your mom was allergic to animals," Mo says. "Why did you use the past tense?"

Tyler's face falls. "She passed away last year. Cancer. It's one of the reasons I moved. I needed to get far away from the hospitals where I spent so much time holding

44

her hand through her treatments. She would have loved Bennett Falls."

"What about your dad?" Mo asks.

"Never met him. My mom raised me on her own. That's how I wound up in a bad neighborhood. We couldn't afford anything else. I had to learn to protect myself and my mom at a young age."

"How so?" Mo asks.

Tyler sits down on the floor opposite the couch, Midnight still purring away in his arms. "When I was ten, this guy knocked on our apartment door. He told my mom to give him all the money she had, or he'd kill us both."

"That's awful," I say, bringing the coffee pot and five mugs on a tray to the coffee table. I sit down between Cam and Mo on the couch.

"She gave him the money, but he didn't think it was enough, so he backhanded her. When I protested, he hit me. Laid me out on the kitchen floor. I still have the scar on the back of my head from where it hit the corner of the kitchen counter on my way down."

"Did you call the police?" Wes asks.

Tyler looks up at Wes. "In my neighborhood, if you called the cops, you'd wind up in a body bag the next day."

"Didn't your mom have any other family? Somewhere she could have taken you?" Mo asks. I can see her tough exterior faltering. She feels sorry for Tyler.

"My mom grew up in foster care. She never knew

who her parents were." The more Tyler talks, the more an accent begins to emerge. Has he been trying to cover it up to blend in better in Bennett Falls?

"What happened after that guy left?" Wes asks. "Did he come back?"

Tyler is quiet for a moment. "I told my mom I'd never let anyone hit her ever again."

"But you were only ten," Mo says. "You couldn't be expected to protect your mom from a guy like that."

"I had no choice. I did what I had to do to survive."

"Which was what?" Cam asks.

"I started picking fights at school with the older kids just so I could get experience throwing punches. I got beat up a lot."

His story is breaking my heart. That is no way for a kid to grow up.

"One day, I picked a fight with the wrong kid. He was playing stick ball with some friends in the street. I watched him, and when he walked home, I jumped on him. Only he had a broom handle from playing stick ball. He swung it at me and broke a few of my ribs. I never told my mom. I just went home, wrapped a pair of her torn panty hose around them and tried not to wince when she was look-ing. But turns out that kid beating me up was a good thing because I learned something important that day."

"Not to pick fights with people?" Mo asks.

"No. Using something like a broom can give you an edge against a stronger opponent."

Midnight's nose twitches in the air, and she finally climbs out of Tyler's lap and walks into the kitchen to eat her dinner.

Tyler stands up. "If you don't mind, I think I'm going to head home now." He looks like he's about to start crying.

"Do you want some crumb cake to go?" Cam asks.

"No, it's okay. Thank you, though. You guys have been really great." He turns to Wes. "You know, after you stopped tackling me."

"Again, I'm really sorry about that," Wes says.

"Don't sweat it. I've taken much worse beatings. I'll see you at work tomorrow," he says to Cam and me.

I walk him to the door. "Hey, are you sure you're okay?"

"Yeah. It's just hard talking about my mom and what my life was like back then." He takes a deep breath and lets it out. "I'll be good, though. See you in the morning." He walks down the hall.

"Jo, your phone is ringing," Mo calls from the couch. "It's a certain incompetent detective. Want me to tell him off?"

"No." I hurry over and grab the phone from the coffee table, bringing it into the kitchen. "What's up, Quentin? I was about to sit down for dessert."

"We have a possible lead on the murder weapon. The medical examiner said it was something long and cylindrical, like a lead pipe or—"

"A broom handle?" The words come rushing out before I even realize I'm saying that.

"Yeah, like that. What made you say that?" he asks.

If I tell him the truth, he'll rush over to Tyler's apartment right now and arrest him. But how do I keep this a secret when Tyler just told us how he learned at the age of ten that a broom handle makes a good weapon to use in a fight?

CHAPTER FIVE

Tuesday morning, I'm still trying to decide what to do about the information I received last night. I didn't tell Quentin about Tyler's story involving the broom handle, and I didn't tell Cam, Wes, and Mo that the medical examiner figured out possible murder weapons either. I knew Mo would jump right back on the "Tyler's guilty" train. But now that it's early morning and only Cam and me in the kitchen of Cup of Jo, I decide it's time to come clean.

"Quentin said the murder weapon is long and cylindrical like a lead pipe or a broom handle." I blurt it all out before I can have second thoughts.

Cam closes the oven and turns to face me. "First, good morning. Second, why are you here so early? And third, why didn't you mention this to me last night?"

"I didn't want to tell you in front of Mo and Wes, but

specifically Mo. I'm here early so we can talk this through. Oh, and good morning." I offer a weak smile.

He walks over and wraps me in a hug. "Did you sleep at all, or did you toss and turn all night stressing out over this?"

"I think I managed to get some sleep, but Midnight did get tired of me keeping her up and insisted on being let out of my apartment around three in the morning."

"Which means you were still up at that time. You should have called me." He pulls back enough to look into my eyes.

"You get up by four so you can come here to bake. I wasn't going to keep you up all night talking." I bob one shoulder. "Besides, one of us has to stay awake today so we can prove Tyler didn't kill Michael Walberg."

"Unless he did. You just gave some pretty compelling evidence to support the theory."

"Except there's no broom. Without the murder weapon, a conviction will be tough."

"How do you want to handle this?" Cam leans back on the island counter behind him. "Do you want to ask Tyler about the broom?"

"I think we have to, right?"

Cam sighs and nods. "We'll do it together, and we'll make sure the broom we use here is locked up in the back office when we do it."

"Are we stupid for allowing Tyler to continue working here during the investigation?"

"You want to give him a paid week off?"

"Maybe we should." Any other employer would probably request a murder suspect kept their distance until the case was closed. Hopefully, paying Tyler for the week off will make him comply without protest or any hard feelings.

Decision made, we finish prepping to open for the day. I have to call both Jamar and Robin in again. Those two can't seem to catch a break. I'll be lucky if one or both don't put in their letters of resignation.

Mrs. Marlow is my first customer of the day. "Good morning, Jo." She cocks her head at me. "What's troubling you?"

"Good morning, Mrs. Marlow. Don't you worry about me. I didn't sleep much last night."

"Well, how could you when you're always chasing after murderers?"

I shouldn't be surprised she knows about my involvement in Quentin's latest case. The woman knows everything that goes on in this town.

"What can I get for you?"

She laughs. "You should know you can't get rid of me that easily, Jo."

"You know I can't talk to you about Quentin's cases," I counter.

"That man. At least we won't have to worry about him for much—" She stops abruptly and waves a hand in the air. "I'll take a large dark roast today."

"No specialty drink?" I ask.

"That Vienna yesterday was delicious, but I'm trying to watch my waistline."

She's not a big woman in any sense of the word, so I'm not sure I buy that excuse. "Are you sure? I'd be happy to make you one."

"Well, okay. You've twisted my arm, Jo. I'll have an elephant ear as well."

"I do believe I saw Cam take some out of the oven a few minutes ago, so they're probably still warm."

"Sounds delightful," she says.

I look up to see Mickey Baldwin walking in. "Just finish your shift at the school, Mickey?" I ask even though I'm well aware he came from work.

"Yes, and I'm starving. Can you double Mrs. Marlow's order for me?"

"You got it. You two go sit, and I'll bring it to you when it's ready." They both have tabs here since they come in every day. It makes it easier for everyone that way.

I prep their drinks and ask Cam to bring me two elephant ears. He made them so big they really do look like elephant ears.

Mickey laughs when I bring them to the table. He holds his up to the side of his head. "Tell Cam he should always make them this big."

"I agree. The bigger, the better," Mrs. Marlow says.

"Enjoy, you two."

Tyler arrives before Jamar or Robin. "Hey, Jo. Can we talk for a minute?"

"Of course." I motion for him to follow me behind the counter so Mickey and Mrs. Marlow can't overhear us. "Is everything okay?"

"Not really. I was thinking. You and Cam have been so great, but I don't want you two to have to deal with people talking behind your backs."

"What do you mean?" I haven't heard any mumbling from customers, so I wasn't under the impression anyone was talking about us.

"It's clear everyone thinks I'm guilty, and I don't want that to affect you and Cam. You've been so nice to me."

My plan to give him a paid week off seems awful now. If Cam and I tell Tyler to stay home, everyone in Bennett Falls will assume we think he's guilty as well. I can't do that to him. Yes, he made himself look bad last night with the story about the broom stick, and it's possible that was his way of confessing without coming right out and saying he's guilty, but I can't bring myself to believe that's true.

"Tyler, you told me you didn't do it. I believe you. Now if there's anything you think I should know, please tell me. Anything at all. Because I'm committed to standing by you through this, but if you're withholding something that will make me look bad in the end..." I shake my head. "I'm going to be really disappointed in you." It would be a weak argument to anyone else, but I know Tyler is eager to please both me and Cam since we're his bosses. I'm counting on the thought of disappointing us being too much for him to bear.

Tyler looks down at his sneakers.

"Why did you tell us about your childhood and having to protect your mom? Did you want us to know about the broomstick for a reason?"

Tyler raises his head and meets my gaze. "I assaulted a man with a broomstick once. It was in self-defense, but I'm sure that detective is going to find out about it, if he hasn't already. I'm not proud of my past, but I did what I had to do. Once I was old enough to get out of there, I did. I wanted to leave that life behind, but it took me a long time to get to that point. And then my mom got sick. I couldn't leave while she was going through that."

"Of course not." I place my hand on his shoulder.

"After she died, I got really angry. She was all I had, and she was gone. This guy tried to mug me on the street after her funeral. I lost it. I grabbed a broom from this guy sweeping his front steps, and I beat the mugger with it. The guy who witnessed the whole thing testified that I was defending myself, so I didn't go to jail."

"But you're worried that the record of that fight will make you seem an even more likely suspect in your roommate's murder," I say.

He swallows so hard I hear it. "Yeah. I'm scared, Jo. I'm afraid to be home alone. I'm afraid of going to prison. All my life, I only wanted to show people that I was worth something. But I'm scared that detective is intent on proving all I'm worthy of is an orange jumpsuit."

Mrs. Marlow steps behind the counter, her gaze

locked on Tyler. "You know what I'm intent on?" she asks.

I have no idea what she's doing or where she's going with this. And Tyler looks even more nervous than I am to hear it.

"I'm intent on showing Quentin Perry that he's an idiot. Now, why don't you come sit at my table for a bit if Jo doesn't need your help right away?"

"Go right ahead," I tell Tyler.

"Are you sure?"

I laugh. "You showed up forty-five minutes early, as usual. Go have some breakfast with Mrs. Marlow. I think you'll both enjoy that."

He smiles at me and extends his arm for Mrs. Marlow to loop hers through. She might be too old to be a mother figure to him, but she'd make an awesome grandmother to anyone. I get another elephant ear and Vienna and bring them to Tyler, who is laughing with Mrs. Marlow and Mickey. Tyler definitely needs Bennett Falls and the people in it.

I go into the kitchen to tell Cam our plan is off. "Tyler has to keep working here through this," I say.

"I saw it all through the window."

"Camden Turner, were you spying?"

"Guilty as charged. I thought you and Mrs. Marlow handled that beautifully."

"Thank you. I think we should go talk to Michael Walberg's girlfriend today. She found the body, and she probably knew the victim best."

"I agree. She's the best one to start with. We should probably follow up with the other neighbors as well. See if anyone else heard or saw anything."

I nod, even though the odds that more than one neighbor was awake that early in the morning aren't that high.

When Jamar and Robin arrive, they come right up to me. "Jo, you should know that some people came in yesterday, saw Tyler, and walked right back out," Jamar says. "Not even my dancing was enough to keep them here."

"I don't care. Tyler is innocent, and I refuse to treat him like a criminal."

Robin bobs her head. "We totally support you. If you trust him, that's enough for me." She motions to Mrs. Marlow, Mickey, and Tyler. "Was that your doing? Because it's smart."

"Actually, Mrs. Marlow did that. She's taken a liking to Tyler."

"She's a good judge of character, so that's saying something right there," Jamar says.

"I thought so, too. Cam and I are going to talk to the victim's girlfriend this morning. If there's any trouble, call me. But you both have the authority to kick people out. If anyone gives you trouble, show them the door, and tell them to take it up with me."

"You got it, boss." Jamar salutes me.

"Should we keep Tyler behind the counter making

drinks and refilling the baked goods displays so he's not interacting with the customers as much?"

"Offer him that option to see if he's more comfortable with it. If he prefers to work with the customers, that's fine. As long as Mrs. Marlow is here, I don't foresee anyone messing with Tyler."

Jamar laughs. "If this were a prison movie, Mrs. Marlow would be the tough crime boss that everyone else listens to."

"I love her to pieces, but I wouldn't put it past that woman to put a hit out on someone," Robin says.

"I wouldn't be surprised if she's the daughter of a mafia boss," Jamar says.

"Daughter?" Mrs. Marlow scoffs behind Jamar, making him jump. "Please, sweetheart, I'd be nothing shy of the boss myself."

I wrap my arm around her.

"Now, you three stop worrying," Mrs. Marlow says. "What Tyler needs is for everyone to act normal."

"You got it," Robin says, heading for the counter.

Jamar reaches for Mrs. Marlow's hand and gently twirls her around.

"Well, if the dancing is already starting, that's my cue to leave." I head for the kitchen to get Cam.

"All set," he says. "Do we have an address for Michael's girlfriend?"

"Hang on." I quickly text Quentin.

I get an almost immediate reply with two addresses, her home and her work. "Judging by the time, I say we start with her work address. She works at the nail salon by the mall. Oh, and her name is Tina Glines."

"Okay, I'll drive since you're operating on virtually no sleep."

It's a good thing Cam drives because the second we're on the road, I pass out in my seat. Cam wakes me up when we get to the salon.

"Sorry I fell asleep on you," I say with a yawn.

"I just wish the ride was longer for you. You were out cold. You obviously needed the sleep."

I unclick my seat belt, and Cam hurries around the SUV to get my door for me. He offers me his arm, and we walk into the salon. The girl at the reception desk looks the right age to be Michael Walberg's girlfriend.

"Hi, we're looking for Tina Glines."

"That's me," she says with a quizzical expression. "I'm not a stylist, though. I only make the appointments."

"We're friends of Tyler Quinn," I say. "Michael's roommate. You're Michael's girlfriend, right?"

"You mean I was." She lowers her head.

"Yes, we're very sorry for your loss," Cam says.

"Thanks. I'm not sure how I feel about it to be honest. I never understood what drew me to Michael in the first place. I mean he couldn't hold a job. He was always getting fired. I paid every time we went out. Just once, I would have loved for him to pick up the check, but it was always, 'You know how it is. It's tough to find good employment.'" She scoffs. "It's not that difficult to show up on time and do the work you're paid to do. I don't know why he didn't understand that."

"Are you saying he'd get fired for not showing up?" I ask.

She shrugs. "I'm assuming that's why he got fired. He's not the responsible type. He'd oversleep or just not show up sometimes. What boss is going to put up with that?"

None. And this proves my theory that Tyler and Michael were polar opposites.

"You found Michael's body yesterday, right?" I ask.

"Yeah. It was awful. There was so much blood."

We saw evidence of that on the carpet in the apartment. "Did you see anything else with blood on it? Something that might have been used to hit Michael?"

"No, but I didn't stay long either. I knew he was dead the second I walked in there. No one loses that much blood and lives to talk about it." She shakes her head. "I backed out of the apartment and called the cops. They made me wait for them to show up, but I refused to go back in there. I told them I only stepped two feet inside. I didn't touch anything but the door. Of course, I'm sure my fingerprints are on other things since I would go there to visit, and Michael wasn't exactly the type to clean."

"Were there any other cars in front of the place when you got there?" Cam asks.

"No, not a one. I figured everyone had gone to work."

"What about Michael's car? Was that there?" I ask.

Tina laughs. "You think he had one? No, I drove him to work. When he went. That's how I know when he went in late or didn't go at all. I don't know what he did before he met me, but that guy didn't have any wheels of his own." She squints at us. "Why are you asking me about him anyway? Who are you really?"

I hold up my hands. "Like I said, we're friends with Tyler. That's all. He's freaking out about this, and we were trying to help him figure out what happened."

She bobs her head. "Yeah, I guess if I was living in that apartment and my roommate was killed, I'd be freaking out, too. I mean, what if the guy who did this comes back for Tyler?"

"Do you know Tyler well?" Cam asks.

"Nah. He seems nice enough, but he's quiet. He makes polite conversation, but he doesn't open up, you know? Still, he was nice to me. Made me coffee in the mornings if I stayed over. Even bought fat free milk for me since he knows I hate that whole milk Michael drank."

"Tyler is thoughtful like that," I say.

"Yeah, I hope he's holding up okay. I probably should have dated him instead. I definitely picked the wrong roommate."

"Why were you at the apartment yesterday? Did you and Michael have plans, or were you taking him to a job interview or something?"

"We were supposed to go to breakfast. He even promised to pay. It's just like him to die to get out of paying the bill." When we don't respond, she says, "That was supposed to be a joke. Sorry. I guess I shouldn't be joking when Michael is dead, but I'm kind of a mess of emotions right now."

"We understand," Cam says. "Grief can be difficult to deal with."

"If I'm being honest, part of me is relieved. You don't know how many times I wanted to hit that guy over the head. Someone else beat me to it." She shakes her head. "Sorry, I'm doing it again."

"Did you notice anything odd about the apartment when you got there? Like anything out of place?" I ask.

"There was one thing, but it's probably nothing."

"What's that?" I ask.

"Well, there was usually a mop hanging on the wall in the kitchen. It was bright green. Like neon colored. I didn't see it."

Could the mop have been used as the murder weapon? It's long and cylindrical like a broom or lead pipe.

"I know what you're talking about," Cam says. "I saw that mop in the kitchen when we were in the apartment."

"Tina you're sure it was gone when you were there?" I ask.

She nods. "I'm positive."

That means the killer was still in the apartment when Tina found the body. They returned the mop after she left and before the police came inside. Then the killer snuck out of the apartment.

"Tina, where were you when you waited for the police to arrive?" I ask.

"In my car. I turned up the music really loud and sang to keep from freaking out."

"Did you see anyone come out of the apartment?" I ask.

"No. I kept my eyes shut until I heard the police sirens."

The killer could have walked right past her.

CHAPTER SIX

A woman walks up behind us. "Excuse me, but I don't want to be late for my nail appointment because you guys are chitchatting." She holds up her right hand. "Do you see what a mess I'm dealing with?"

"I'm so sorry, Ms. Cooper," Tina says. "You can go right to Tiffany's station. I'll sign you in."

The woman gives a curt nod and hurries off.

"We're sorry we've taken up so much of your time," Cam tells Tina. "Thank you for speaking with us."

She looks like she has more she wants to say, so I don't make any move to leave. "I always sort of suspected Michael was mixed up in some bad stuff."

"Like what?" I ask.

Tina bites her bottom lip and seems to be contemplating if she should tell us. "He could be secretive. Like I once asked where he was from, and his answers didn't line up. One time he was from a small town out west, and another time he said he grew up in a big city. When I asked him about it, he said he was a private person and his past was his alone." She lets out a shaky breath. "He could be a little scary at times, so I dropped the matter."

Was she afraid of him? "Tina, I hope you don't mind me asking, but why did you stay with Michael? It seems like you questioned quite a few things about him."

She looks around the salon. "I don't have family here. My sister and I grew up with our aunt and uncle after our parents died in a car accident. They took us in out of obligation, and they never acted like our parents. When we turned eighteen, they said it was time for us to move out and get jobs and lives of our own. My sister met a great guy and got married by the time she turned twenty. I wound up here, dating one loser after another. I have terrible taste in men. I guess I kept hoping one of them would be different." She shakes her head. "Can I ask you something?"

"Of course," I say.

"Do you think I'm in danger? The thing with the mop. You said you saw it in the apartment, but how is that possible unless..." She bites her lip again. "The killer was still there, wasn't he?"

"We don't know that for sure. It's possible the police found the mop somewhere else and hung it up," I say, knowing they wouldn't jeopardize the crime scene like that, but I can tell Tina is scared, so I'm trying to calm her down. "Maybe you should plan a trip to see your sister for a little while, though. It might make you feel better to spend time with family and to get away from here for a while."

"Yeah, maybe you're right."

Another customer walks in, so Cam and I say goodbye to Tina.

Once we're back on the road, I say, "It's so scary to think Tina was in the apartment while the killer was still there."

"Yeah, and how do you think he got out without being seen?"

Tina already explained that the killer could have gotten past her since she had her eyes closed, but what about the other neighbors? I'm not sure the killer would risk walking right out the front door. "Let's go back to the apartment. I want to talk to the other neighbors and see if there is another way out of the apartment."

"Are you going to call Quentin?" Cam asks. "He should really have the CSI team check out the mop hanging in the kitchen. There's a good chance the killer used it."

"But why would he?" Most mops are cheap plastic, which pretty much rules it out as a possible murder weapon because it would break before it could actually do damage to anyone.

Cam doesn't have an answer, so we sit in silence as we think. By the time we get to the apartment, I have a possible theory, but I need to be inside the apartment to test it out. Looks like I need to call Quentin after all. I pull out my phone.

Quentin's hello comes out more as a yawn than an actual word.

"Can you meet Cam and me at Tyler and Michael's apartment. We're here now, and I think we might have some evidence for you." I hear his siren come on and realize he's on the road.

"I was on my way back to the station, but I'll go to the apartment instead. Fill me in on what you've got."

I tell him about our conversation with Tina Glines.

"This is bad. If the killer knows Tina was there, she's in danger."

"I told her to go visit her sister for a while to get out of town."

"She needs police protection, Jo. She could be a witness."

"Even though she didn't see anything?"

"She saw the mop was missing. That puts the killer in the apartment at that time."

"And clears Tyler Quinn since he was at Cup of Jo," I say with a smile.

"If your theory is correct, yes. But I'm not crossing off any suspects until I figure out if that's true.

The sound of sirens fills the air as Cam parks in front of Tyler's apartment, which means Quentin is close. When he pulls up next to us, I disconnect the call and step out of the vehicle.

Quentin brings us upstairs and unlocks the door. The place looks the same, like nothing has been touched.

"Where is Tyler staying?" I ask.

"In a cheap motel," Quentin says. "We asked him not to disturb anything here until we're able to get concrete evidence. He complied with our request."

"So he's being cooperative," I say.

"Yes. I'll give him that much." Quentin points to the mop hanging in the kitchen. "There it is. Just like it was when we arrived on the scene."

"Do you remember if it was wet?" I ask.

He gives me a look. "There was a dead body and you think I took notice of whether or not the mop had recently been used?"

"What about the kitchen floor? Was it wet?"

Quentin huffs and crosses his arms. "What are you getting at, Jo? You think the killer is a neat freak and decided to do some housework while he was here?"

I roll my eyes. "No, I'm thinking the killer got some blood on him and tracked it into the kitchen."

"If he stepped in the blood, there would have been bloody footprints on the carpet in the living room." He gestures to the carpeting. "As you can see, there aren't."

"Okay, but what if the blood that was tracked into the kitchen wasn't from the killer's shoe? It could have been on the killer's arm or hand? Or maybe it dripped from the murder weapon."

"Why would he come into the kitchen in the first place?" Quentin asks.

Cam holds out a hand, indicating he has an idea. "Tina said she suspected Michael was into some shady things. What if he was dealing drugs, and the killer knew Michael hid his stash in the kitchen?"

I point to Cam. "And when he went to get it, he dripped blood onto the floor and cleaned it up using the mop hanging on the wall."

"Or the mop was the murder weapon," Quentin says.

"I'm not sure the killer would have left it behind if that were the case." It would have made more sense to take the murder weapon so the police didn't have one to use at a trial. "Besides, look at that mop. It would have broken if someone tried to use it as a weapon."

"Okay." Quentin draws out the word. "So you think the killer was cleaning up the blood in the kitchen when Tina arrived."

I nod. "He probably had the mop in hand, so he hid in one of the bedrooms until she left."

"How did he get out then if she was waiting outside for the police to arrive?" Quentin asks.

Seriously, do I have to do all of his work for him? I walk past him to Michael's bedroom. "There's a window," I say.

"You think he jumped out a second-story window?" Quentin's tone makes it clear how idiotic he believes that theory to be.

"What I think is you're supposed to be the police detective, yet you haven't done any detective work at all."

I glare at him before walking to the window. Looking out it, I have to agree that it's not likely the killer jumped from here. I turn around and walk out of the room. There is one other option. I go into Tyler's room.

When I see the door leading to a balcony, I stop short. "You knew this was here."

Quentin bobs his head.

"You let me find it because you knew I'd jump down your throat if you suggested the killer was Tyler and he left the house from his own bedroom balcony."

"What can I say? I know you well."

Cam uses his elbow to open the balcony door, careful not to get fingerprints on the door handle. We step outside to see there is a set of stairs leading from what I thought was a balcony but is actually a tiny back deck.

"And now you know how the killer got out without being seen from the front of the house," Quentin says. "Still think your new employee is so innocent?"

"This doesn't prove anything," I say. "The killer could have gotten lucky by hiding in this bedroom and stumbling across an escape route."

"Sure, and I could have gotten lucky and won the lottery last week, but I'm positive neither happened." Quentin grabs his phone from his pocket. "This is Detective Perry. I need the CSI team back at the crime scene. I have a mop and a balcony that need to be tested for prints or any other DNA."

He knows he'll find Tyler's prints on both. All I can

do now is hope the killer was careless enough not to wear gloves. But something tells me I'm not going to be that lucky. And neither is Tyler. Quentin is going to have enough evidence to hold Tyler for murder.

CHAPTER SEVEN

While Quentin and the CSI team do their thing inside Tyler's apartment, Cam and I head downstairs to knock on the neighbors' doors.

"Did you see the smug look he gave me as we walked out of the apartment?" I ask Cam as we walk downstairs. "I swear he thinks he's finally beaten me to finding the murderer."

"It's not often he even gets to think he's one-upped you. Try not to let it get to you. When he figures out he's been wrong all along, you'll get the last laugh."

More like everyone in Cup of Jo will get the last laugh when Mickey tells the story to all my customers. He thrives on being the first to spread the news of me solving Quentin's cases for him. Sometimes I wonder how Quentin can stand living in this town when most of the residents have turned on him. I've tried to get them to be a little nicer to Quentin, but it's not easy to help a man who is constantly putting me in bad situations.

A young woman pulls up in a blue Honda Civic and parks in front of the apartment right below Tyler and Michael's.

"Excuse me," I call to her. "Do you live here?"

She eyes me skeptically as she gets out of the car. "Yeah. Why are the police here again? Did something else happen?"

"No. Everything is fine," I say. "Do you know the residents who live in the apartment above you?"

She fishes her keys out of her pocket and starts for the door. "Not really. I don't talk to anyone who lives here. This is just temporary until I find a better place. I'm not looking to make friends."

"So you didn't know Michael Walberg then?" I ask.

"Saw his face on the news, but that's about it." She unlocks her door and heads inside, closing it in our faces.

I knock. "Please, we just have a few questions for you."

The door swings open. "I don't have any answers for you. You're wasting your time."

"Did you hear anything coming from the apartment above yours Monday morning?"

"Of course. I heard that jerk's music. He always plays it too loud. He has absolutely no consideration for anyone else who lives here."

"You heard the music yesterday morning? You're sure?" I ask.

"Yeah, I'm sure. It woke me up. I don't have any classes on Mondays, so it should be my day to sleep in. Except that's impossible with inconsiderate neighbors."

It's odd how she's still complaining about the guy when she's well aware that he's dead. "Do you know what time that was?"

"A little after seven."

That means Michael was alive well after Tyler got to Cup of Jo. Quentin must have questioned this girl, so why is he still so insistent on keeping Tyler as his prime suspect? "Did you have any communication with Michael Walberg? You know, like asking him to turn his music down?"

"I banged on the ceiling with the broom, but he didn't get the hint."

With a broom? It's still possible that was the murder weapon. "Did you go up there with the broom?" I ask, and Cam meets my gaze.

"No. You can't reason with stupidity. I thought banging might get through to him. I was wrong. So I got up and took a shower to start my day."

"Then you didn't see anyone else come to the apartment complex?" Cam asks.

"Nope."

"Did you hear anyone else in the apartment above yours?" I ask.

"I only heard the music."

I wonder if the music was on when the police arrived. Neither Quentin nor Tina mentioned it to us when we spoke to them about finding the body. If the killer turned off the music, it's possible his prints are on the device that was playing it. But it's probably more likely that Michael turned off the music when he answered the door.

"Like I said, I have no answers for you. Now I have schoolwork to do. If I don't finish this degree, I'll never get a nicer place than this, and after the murder, I'm a little eager to get out of here."

"Thank you for your time," Cam says as she closes the door in our faces again.

"Still here?" Quentin asks, coming down the stairs.

"Was there music playing in the apartment when you first arrived at the crime scene?" I ask him.

"No. Why?"

"Because this neighbor told us Michael's music woke her up around seven o'clock."

"Grace Clark. She's a ball of sunshine, isn't she?"

"Did she tell you she banged on the floor with a broom to try to get Michael to turn down the music?"

"I doubt she'd divulge that information if she then used the broom to beat Michael to death, so if that's what you're hinting at, I'd say you're way off base."

"Did you notice what time she said it was? Seven. Tyler was with Cam and me at seven, so if Michael was still alive, Tyler isn't the killer."

Quentin sighs. "Okay, look, Jo, I get what you're saying, but no one spoke to Michael after Tyler left. Tyler could have set an alarm to start playing music at seven o'clock so it would seem like Michael was still alive. It's not like that's difficult to do."

"And how would the music turn off on its own then?"

"I don't know. Maybe Michael got a phone call, and it interrupted the alarm."

I shake my head. "Who lives in the other downstairs apartment?"

Quentin pulls his notepad from his pocket. "Hector Greene. He's a sanitation worker. He left for work at four in the morning."

Which means he wasn't home when Michael Walberg was murdered.

"The team is taking the mop back to the lab, but initial tests show traces of blood and bleach."

"Can you test the blood to see if its Michael's?" I ask.

"That's the plan. So far the only prints on anything belong to Michael and Tyler."

"Then this was premeditated. The killer wore gloves because he knew he was going to commit murder."

"Or it's—"

"We were with Tyler!" I yell. "Why do you think we're lying to you to cover for him? Come on, Quentin."

"I don't think you're lying, Jo. I think you aren't seeing things clearly because you care about your employee, which doesn't make a whole lot of sense considering you barely know him."

"More like I see people as human beings, while you see them as a means to an end."

"What is that supposed to mean?" he asks.

"It means you only care about closing the case. Why are you so eager to wrap this up anyway? What is the rush?"

He looks off into the distance.

"Is it Quentin Junior? Did something happen and you want to get to the hospital to be with him?" He really should consider taking a leave of absence. Ever since his son was born, he's been unable to focus on anything else.

"I'm following the evidence. It happens to lead back to your employee every time. That's not my fault."

"Did you find any evidence of drugs in the apartment?" I ask. "Have you looked into the possibility that this was a drug deal gone bad?"

"There's no sign of drugs anywhere. I'm not going to waste time on a wild goose chase. I'm calling Tyler Quinn back down to the station."

I can't believe this. I swear he just wants to make my life miserable. How is it possible that we keep ending up at odds with each other?

"I'm sorry, Jo, but hopefully, this will be over soon, and we won't have to—" He shakes his head and walks toward his patrol car.

"What was that about?" Cam asks.

"I'm not sure, but I don't understand much about Quentin."

"We can't stop him from interrogating Tyler, so what can we do to help? Should we go to the station to be there for Tyler?"

Like Cam said, we can't stop Quentin from questioning him. I think our best bet is to find the real killer since Quentin's clearly not interested in doing that. "We need to dig into Michael Walberg more and find out what he was doing that would get him killed."

"You want to go see Mo and Wes."

I know they're working, but if Mo can point Cam and me in the right direction, we might be able to find something on our own. I nod, and we get back into Cam's SUV.

Mo closes the door to her office. "You guys, this is going to be crazy hard. None of the social media profiles I found for Michael Walberg match the victim."

"How is it possible for someone to have no online footprint?" Cam asks. "I'm not big on social media, but even I turn up on a few sites. Mostly because of Cup of Jo."

"Yeah, well, Michael wasn't a model employee," Mo says. "The guy couldn't hold a job, right?"

"Tina said he worked for a gas station for a little while."

"There won't be any record of that online," Mo says.

"Do we go around to all the gas stations and show his picture to the people who work there?" Cam asks.

"That could take all day." I groan in frustration.

"I can make you a list of all the Michael Walbergs, but it will most likely overwhelm you," Mo says.

"Quentin has the guy's fingerprints, right? Maybe he needs to run them through the system so we can get a better idea of who we're dealing with."

"Sure, I'll call him right now and tell him to stop wasting his time interrogating Tyler and start figuring out who the victim really was. I can just imagine he'll drop everything to listen to me." My sarcasm is so thick I can practically feel it in the air between us.

"What we need is a friend at the BFPD, not someone who likes to enlist your help but dismiss all your ideas until you hand him a conviction on a silver platter."

"We'd have better luck going to the medical examiner and pretending Quentin sent us to get information for him."

Mo's eyes light up. "Or, we can contact the medical examiner as Quentin."

"Pretending to be an officer of the law is a felony, Mo." I shake my head. "Quentin would love a reason to put you in handcuffs. You give him a harder time than anyone else in town."

"No way. He wouldn't risk losing your help to arrest me, no matter how much joy the actual act of putting me behind bars would give him." She waves a hand in the air. "Besides, I'm not afraid of Quentin Perry."

"How about Chief Harvey?" I ask her. "He'd arrest you, too."

"Fine, then let's email the medical examiner and ask for the information. We'll tell him Quentin is busy with a suspect at the moment. That part is true."

It might work, especially if we never actually say Quentin asked us to do it. "Let me write the email. I'd rather you be able to honestly say you didn't write it."

She stands up from her desk so I can use her computer. I pull up my email and realize I don't have the ME's contact information.

"Here." Mo places her phone on the desk next to the keyboard. "I found the email address for you."

I type it into the address bar and begin writing. I mention that Quentin is interrogating his top suspect and that I'm trying to gather more information on the victim for him. That should make it sound like he asked me to do this without coming out and actually lying. I ask for the fingerprint analysis and all information confirming the victim's identity. I also mention how common the name is and how we are being careful that we're looking into the correct person. Hopefully, this is enough to get me a response and soon. Once I'm finished, I send the email and stand up.

"We should check in at work," Cam says.

"I agree. I don't want Jamar or Robin quitting on us after we promised to start giving them days off." We've actually needed them more than usual lately. I can't imagine either one of them is happy about that.

"I'll keep looking into Michael Walberg on my breaks," Mo says. "I'll call if I find anything."

"Thanks, Mo."

"Oh, and next time, stop at Cup of Jo first. You didn't even bring me coffee." She shakes her head.

"I'll ask Jamar to deliver some for you and Wes."

"With some more of that banana hazelnut crumb cake. It's my new addiction."

I wind up delivering their food and drinks because I don't have the heart to ask Jamar to make deliveries when he shouldn't even be working today to begin with. Weekends are too busy, so until Tyler is cleared of murder charges and learns the ropes at Cup of Jo, I need to keep Jamar and Robin on for weekends. I planned to give them Mondays and Tuesdays off for a while instead.

"Is it true Tyler was called back in for questioning?" Mickey asks me after I get back from delivering Mo's and Wes's goodies.

"Mickey, shouldn't you be at home asleep?"

"I'll go, but I heard a rumor that someone saw Tyler's car at the station. I figured you'd know what that was about." He smiles at me, eagerly awaiting my response.

"I haven't been down to the station, so I can neither confirm nor deny."

"Oh, come on, Jo." Mickey's voice couldn't be any whinier. "If I go home to bed and something big happens, it's going to ruin my reputation."

"Maybe you need a new reputation," I say over my shoulder as I head behind the counter.

"Maybe I need a new hangout to conduct my business."

I whirl around on him. "Don't let me stop you," I say, calling his bluff.

"Okay, fine. We both know that was an empty threat, but you have to give me something."

"I can't. I'm not even really sure who the victim was. We know nothing about him except that he couldn't seem to hold a job for more than a few weeks."

"Do you know where he worked?" Mickey asks.

"His last known job was at a gas station in town, but we don't even know which one."

Mickey purses his lips and looks up at the ceiling. "Gas station, huh? The one by the high school has a big turnover rate. It's like there's a different worker every week or so."

"You saw Michael Walberg's photo on TV, right?" I ask.

Mickey nods.

"Did he look familiar to you?"

"Maybe. I'm not sure. You know I'm exhausted when I leave work. I don't perk up until I get here for my caffeine fix."

Yeah, his daily caffeine fix before he goes home to bed. Mickey's entire life is pretty much the opposite of the rest of the population's. But maybe I can help jog his memory. "That's too bad." I tsk for added effect. "Imagine if the break in this case is you telling me—and the police by extension—that you recognized the murder victim from the gas station." I wave a hand in the air. "Oh well. It's probably for the best anyway. Who would want that kind of attention?"

The answer to that question is Mickey. He thrives on

being the center of attention. It's the reason he became the town gossip.

He wags a finger in the air. "You know, I think I do remember that guy from the gas station. Yeah, he worked in the little convenience store there. I had trouble with the pump one day and had to go in to pay."

"That's great, Mickey. Thanks."

"Happy to help. Are you and Cam going to head there now?"

"That's the plan." I kiss his cheek before running into the kitchen to tell Cam the good news.

We pull up to the gas station, and park in one of the spots directly in front of the convenience store. There's a girl working behind the counter. She has a long blonde ponytail that's braided in tons of tiny sections. She looks up at us. "Is it pump three? It's been acting up for months now."

"No, we're actually here to find out if Michael Walberg used to be an employee."

"No clue. I just started last week."

That means she could have been hired to replace Michael. "Oh, I think he was let go right around that time."

"Wait. You're talking about that guy?" She jerks her head back.

"Then you do know him," I say.

"More like I know of him. He stole from the cash register, and my boss fired him. From what the other workers told me, Mr. Little was livid."

"Really?" Cam asks. "Did they fight about it?"

"I heard Mr. Little chased that guy out of here with the metal bar he puts in the door at night for added safety."

That gives Mr. Little motive and a possible match for the murder weapon. I look at the girl working the register. "Is your boss around?" If Mr. Little and Michael Walberg fought over stolen money, there's a good chance it didn't end with Mr. Little chasing Michael out of the convenience store.

"Um, I'm not sure. I can call him, though." She picks up her phone from the countertop, and after a few taps of her screen, she brings the phone to her ear. "Mr. Little, there are some people here asking about that guy you fired." She pauses. "Yeah, they're here now." Her eyes widen. "Why?"

The squeal of tires in the parking lot draws my attention.

"Are you driving?" the girl says into her phone.

I hurry to the door to see a black Camaro tearing out of the parking lot. "He's running away!"

CHAPTER EIGHT

Cam and I rush back to his SUV. The good news is I know what Mr. Little is driving since I saw him flee, but the bad news is the man is driving like a maniac and has a head start on us. I call Quentin.

"This better be good. I just got to the hospital to visit with Quentin Junior," he answers.

"We're following a suspect. Mr. Little was Michael Walberg's boss at the gas station by the high school. Michael stole money from him, and Mr. Little chased him out of the station with a metal bar. When Little found out we were here asking questions, he ran."

Cam changes lanes quickly, and I nearly slam my head into the window. "Jo, are you okay? I'm so sorry. He turned at the last minute."

"I'm okay. Quentin, he just turned into the mall. I think he's trying to lose us in the crowd of people." It would be a better plan if it was the weekend. Tuesdays aren't nearly as busy of shopping days since most people are at work.

Quentin groans. "Don't do anything stupid. You don't know if this guy is armed, and he's clearly guilty of something. I'm on my way." He stays on the line in case we have any updates on where Little went, but he's quiet other than his breathing. It sounds like he's gritting his teeth and breathing out his mouth. I can imagine how angry he is to miss out on time with his son for this case.

Little's car cuts behind the row of restaurants on the outskirts of the mall. Cam follows and narrowly makes it around a large dumpster without hitting it.

"Jo, this is too dangerous. I'm not going to get us killed to do Quentin's police work." Cam slows to a stop. "I'm not sure which way he went anyway."

I'm pretty sure Little looped around the restaurants, but Cam is right. His SUV isn't really a high-speed chase vehicle, and we don't have badges, which means we could get pulled over for reckless driving as well. "Quentin, we lost him."

"I'll call you back," he says.

"What do you think he's doing?" Cam asks, easing the SUV back onto the road that leads around the mall.

"Probably trying to get a BOLO out on Little's car." We don't have his resources, but we do have Mo. I dial her on speaker.

"Hey, Jo," she answers.

"Can you find out the full name and contact information for the man who owns the gas station by the high school? His last name is Little."

"Where are you?" she asks. "It sounds like you're in the car."

"I am. Cam and I chased Little in his Camaro to the mall parking lot. He lost us, so I have Quentin trying to get us some help."

"I see." Her "I see" sounds more like a "challenge accepted."

"This isn't a race to see if you can find this guy before the BFPD does, Mo."

"Sure. But when I do, I'm still going to laugh and claim my victory." Her fingers are flying across her keyboard so fast it sounds like little elves tap dancing. "Okay, Victor Little. He drives a black Chevy Camaro. Oh, he lives by the mall. There's an apartment complex behind it. Looks like Victor owns it and lives there as well. He's in apartment thirteen B."

"You're the best, Mo. Thanks."

"Be sure to tell Quentin. Good luck, and be careful."

"We will." I end the call, and Cam is already driving toward the apartment complex, which is visible from the parking lot. "I'm guessing Little will ditch his car in the mall parking lot and run from there."

"You think his plan was to park behind the restaurants and go on foot?" Cam asks.

"Most likely. He probably thought you wouldn't follow him back there in the SUV." The spaces behind the restaurants are really cramped. Trucks making deliveries usually pull up in front while the establishments are closed still.

"He might be trying to grab some things and make a run for it now that he knows we're on to him."

It does make sense that he would leave. It's too easy to track him to his house. Mo did it in a matter of minutes. Of course, Mo would probably make a really impressive intelligence agent if the government ever got wind of her computer skills.

"Why do you think he stuck around to begin with?" I ask.

"He probably thought no one would suspect him. If the workers at the gas station were the only ones who witnessed Little chasing Walberg out, they probably thought Little was just defending his business. And the police haven't released any information about how Walberg was killed, so no one would suspect the metal pipe Little had could be the murder weapon."

But Victor Little now knows that Cam and I have more information than the general public. He might not have seen us in person, but I'm sure we're on camera. I bet the entire gas station and convenience store are monitored by cameras, and those are most likely connected to Victor Little's phone. It's probably how he caught Michael Walberg stealing. Which begs the question, why didn't he take that video footage to the police to get his money back? Why would Little decide to kill Walberg instead? There must be more going on here.

My phone rings, and Quentin's name pops up on my screen. "We're at Victor Little's apartment," I tell him.

"Do not approach him, Jo. I'm pulling into the mall parking lot now. I'll be at the apartment in about two minutes." He pauses. "Did Mo get the address for you?"

"There's nothing she can't do," I say.

"Does she want a job at the BFPD?" he jokes.

I laugh because no amount of money in the world could sway Mo to work with Quentin. She hates him so much you'd think he cheated on her, not me.

Quentin parks next to us and gets out. Cam and I meet him in front of our vehicles. "What's the plan?" I ask.

"You two stay here. We don't know if Little has a gun in there."

"If he did, why didn't he shoot Michael Walberg?" I ask.

"Because bullets can be traced back to the shooter. You said he chased Walberg with a metal pipe?"

"Yeah, one of the gas station employees said it was a metal bar Little puts in the door for added security after locking it."

Quentin nods. "Like people putting bars in their sliding glass doors so no one can break the lock and come in. The bar prevents the door from sliding open at all."

"Exactly. And it fits the MO of the murder weapon."

Quentin furrows his brow at me. "I guess it shouldn't surprise me to hear you talk like that after…" He shakes his head, not wanting to talk about our past relationship in front of Cam. "Anyway, you stay here. I'm going to knock on the door."

Quentin has one hand on the gun holstered to his hip as he makes his way to apartment thirteen B. Apparently the B means it's on the second floor, and being an odd number places it on the left side of the building. I find it interesting that the numbers don't go in order. They skip so their even counterparts are on the right side of the building. I wonder who came up with that idea.

Quentin bangs a fist on the door. "Victor Little, this is the Bennett Falls Police. Open up!" His voice is commanding and loud.

I'm not surprised when the door doesn't open.

"Mr. Little, I know you're inside. You can open up now, or I can come back with a warrant for your arrest. This is your last chance to choose to cooperate."

Out of the corner of my eye, I see movement at the end of the building. I grab Cam's hand and tug in that direction. His gaze discreetly goes to the side of the building.

"I see him," Cam says, barely moving his mouth in the process.

"Can you tell if he has a weapon?" I ask, turning my head slightly toward Cam so Little can't see that I'm talking.

"I'm not sure." Cam wraps his arm around me and walks me to the driver's side of the SUV to keep the vehicle positioned between us and Little.

Quentin pounds on the door again, and Little makes

his move. He rushes toward a white beat-up pickup truck parked at the end of the lot. He's carrying a duffle bag but no weapon that I can see.

"We can't let him get away," I tell Cam.

Cam grabs my arm to hold me in place. "Quentin!"

Quentin turns toward us, and Cam points to the truck, which is now backing out of the parking space. Quentin raises his gun and fires, shooting the front driver's side tire. He runs down the stairs and right to the truck.

Victor Little tries to drive, but Quentin blocks his path, the gun aimed right at the windshield. "Stop the vehicle and get out with your hands in the air!"

"You're going to pay to replace that tire," Little says, putting the truck in park and stepping out.

"You were evading the police," Quentin says. "On your knees with your hands behind your head. Now! You're under arrest."

"For what?"

"The murder of Michael Walberg."

"I didn't kill anyone," Victor says. "This is crazy. I want my lawyer."

"That's the smartest move you've made yet." Quentin cuffs him and pulls him to his feet. He looks at me as he brings Victor to his patrol car. "Meet me at the station."

Sometimes, it feels even stranger to have Quentin ask for my help than it does for him to tell me to stay out of police business.

Cam and I don't rush to the station since Victor Little

requested his lawyer be present for questioning. We stop in Cup of Jo to make sure everything is under control.

"We're fine, Jo, really," Robin says. "It's not your fault this happened. And honestly, I feel awful that Tyler is dealing with this. He seems so nice."

"How is he doing?" My gaze goes to Tyler, who is wiping down a table in the corner.

"As well as he can be. Mrs. Marlow is keeping a close eye on him. She's been here all day."

"She sweet to look after him."

"She told me he reminds her of her grandson."

I question if I should send Tyler home so he can rest, but the thought of sitting in a hotel room alone seems depressing to me. I'm not sure he'd want to leave, and I certainly don't want him to think I'm questioning his innocence. I squeeze Robin's arm before walking over to Tyler.

"Hey, Tyler. I have a question for you."

He slings the dish rag over his right shoulder. "Sure. Go ahead."

"Do you know Victor Little?"

Tyler squints as he tries to recall the name. "I don't think so. Why?"

"He was Michael's boss at the gas station."

"Oh. Okay, then yeah. He talked about his boss but never by name."

"Did Michael complain about him or mention any problems with him?"

"No. He said the guy was rarely ever there because

he managed some properties in the area as well as the gas station. Michael only told me that because I asked how he still had a job when he overslept so much." Tyler bobs one shoulder. "He said his boss wasn't ever around to notice, and none of his coworkers were snitches."

"What did Michael do at the gas station? It's self-service."

"He worked the register in the convenience store. I guess someone else was usually on shift with him."

The girl we spoke with was telling the truth then. She was hired after Michael was fired. But she was working alone. I wonder what happened to whoever it was who worked with Michael. Did Victor Little fire him or her, too?

"Hey, just so you know, if you need to take a break, you can go back to your hotel room whenever you need. Robin and Jamar can handle things here."

Tyler looks over at them at the counter, talking to customers. "I appreciate you not firing me or insisting I take time off. It's easier to be here than sitting in that hotel room. But if you want me to go so you don't have to pay three people to do the job of two, I get it."

"Don't worry about that. I'll let Jamar and Robin know one of them can go home if they'd like the day off." I smile at Tyler before going to the counter.

"Hey, you guys."

Jamar holds up a hand. "Don't even think about telling us we can take the rest of the day off. We're not leaving."

I laugh. "Need the extra cash?"

"Oh." Robin presses a hand to her mouth. "I didn't even think that it's costing you more money to have all three of us working."

I hold up my hand to stop her. "Don't worry about that. I promised you days off. The least I can do is pay you overtime."

"Overtime?" Robin asks. "No, that's not necessary, Jo. Really."

"I insist. You guys are really helping us out, and you're helping Tyler, too."

"He's a good guy," Jamar says. "He reminds me of Lance."

That gets Robin's attention since she's currently dating our mutual friend Lance. "How so?"

"When Jo met Lance, he was really down on his luck. Then he came into that inheritance and things worked out well for him with his restaurant. But he was accused of murdering the guy who gave him the inheritance."

"Lance was accused of murder?" Robin shakes her head. "He never told me."

"Probably because it was completely absurd and all Quentin's fault," I say. "You know how he likes to accuse anyone who is remotely connected to the victim. Like in this case with Tyler and Michael."

"Oh, now I see what you mean, Jamar," Robin says. "Poor Lance. I never knew Quentin put him through this."

"I'm sure he doesn't like to talk about it," I say. I

wonder if Lance told Robin his mother is in jail. Lance has a few skeletons in his closet, but he's such a sweet guy.

"Jo, we should get going," Cam says. "I refilled the display cases, and there's a tray of cream puffs in the kitchen," he tells Robin and Jamar.

"Great. Do you need us to close up tonight?" Jamar asks.

I look at the clock on the wall, which is made up of coffee cups where the numbers should be. The day has completely gotten away from us. "Would you mind?"

"We've got it," Robin says.

"You guys are the best. Thank you."

Tyler stops us before we can leave. "I thought of something. You said the guy from the gas station is named Victor, right?"

"Yeah. Why?"

"Well, I heard Tina on the phone one day. She mentioned someone named Victor. I think she knew him. Pretty well. I think they might have dated at some point."

Did Tina leave Victor Little for Michael? That would give Victor another reason to want Michael dead.

CHAPTER NINE

We say goodbye to Tyler and head to the station. Quentin is waiting for us at his desk.

"Victor Little's lawyer is his cousin, Timothy Little." Quentin clamps his lips together like he's trying not to laugh.

"Tiny Tim," I say.

Quentin bobs his head.

"What?" Cam asks.

"Quentin is trying not to laugh because the name Timothy Little makes him think of Tiny Tim from *A Christmas Carol*. He always liked the Disney version." I have to tell Quentin what Tyler said about Tina Glines and Victor Little. "Quentin, according to Tyler, Michael's girlfriend was dating Victor Little at some point. I don't know if they were still seeing each other or if she left him for Michael, but there's something there."

"Yeah, we call that motive." Quentin clears his

throat. "I'm thinking Tyler may have caught a break here. Victor had motive, means, and opportunity to kill Walberg. We might close this case today."

I'd love that, but a thought pops into my head. "I just realized something," I say.

"What?" Cam turns to face me. "Michael Walberg was hit from behind."

"Yeah? So?" Quentin shrugs.

"Well, that means he let the killer into his apartment. He wouldn't have let Victor Little inside. Not after they fought at the gas station and Victor chased him with a metal bar. And definitely not if they were fighting over Tina. I'm guessing Walberg would have slammed the door in his face if he opened it at all."

"Little could have forced his way in," Quentin says.

"Okay, for argument sake, let's say he did. In what situation would you turn your back on your attacker?"

"If you're trying to run away," Quentin says as if the answer is so obvious a preschooler would see it.

"To where? He'd run out the door, not into the apartment."

"There's the deck off Tyler's room," Quentin says. "Maybe he was going there."

"That seems highly unlikely to me. If someone comes at you with a weapon, isn't your natural instinct to defend yourself?"

"Or grab for the weapon," Cam says. "Did the medical examiner find any defensive wounds on the body?"

Quentin shakes his head.

"Then Michael Walberg didn't grab for the weapon or try to deflect a hit." I shake my head. "He let this person into the apartment and didn't feel threatened by them."

"You don't know that, Jo."

"It makes sense."

"Not much is logical when it comes to murder."

Okay, so killing someone isn't a logical or rational response to a disagreement, but human instinct is typically logical and rational. At least when it comes to life-threatening situations. It's the fight-or-flight response. I don't dare say that, though, because Quentin will tell me that proves Michael tried to run from his attacker and was struck from behind as a result. Something isn't sitting right with me there.

"Victor Little isn't the biggest man," I say.

Quentin scoffs. "Yeah, I'm willing to bet he got teased a lot, especially since his last name fits his stature."

"So how then did he force his way into Michael Walberg's apartment? And why would Walberg run from him instead of fighting?"

"What if Walberg decided to return the money he stole so Little wouldn't press charges?" Cam asks. "They might have arranged to meet at the apartment so Walberg could give Little the money without the authorities getting involved."

Quentin points a finger at Cam. "Yeah, and Little

didn't want to tell us that because it put him at the crime scene the morning of the murder."

I hold up a hand. "Wait. Are you two agreeing with each other?"

Cam bobs one shoulder. "I'm just trying to think of all the possibilities. I'm not saying that's what happened."

"I think it's time to talk to Victor," I say. "We need answers."

Quentin brings us to the interrogation room. The first thing I notice is how Timothy Little towers over his cousin. He's not tiny by any means.

"Who are you people?" Victor asks, and Timothy holds up a hand to silence him.

"I'll do the talking, Victor." Timothy Little laces his fingers on the table, and I get the impression he's trying to show us he's at ease. "I would like to know who you are and why you're part of this questioning."

"I'm Joanna Coffee, and this is my fiancé and business partner, Camden Turner. We run Cup of Jo on Main Street."

"Good for you. Now why are you here?" Timothy's tone makes it clear he's not impressed with us or our coffee shop.

"Ms. Coffee and Mr. Turner are consultants on this case," Quentin says.

Timothy Little laughs. "Consultants? If you'd said caterers that would have made more sense. What on earth can two coffee shop owners possibly offer to a police investigation other than some caffeine and baked goods?"

Victor joins his cousin in laughing at our expense.

I raise a hand slightly, letting Quentin know I've got this. "Well, the victim's roommate happens to be one of our employees. We've also discovered that Victor here had an altercation with the victim over some money taken from the cash register at the gas station. Not to mention Michael Walberg was dating Tina Glines, who is also connected to Mr. Little." I gesture to him for added emphasis. "And the metal bar that you threatened Michael Walberg with at the gas station seems to be a match for the object used to murder Walberg."

"Interesting theory," Timothy Little says.

"Isn't it, though?" I ask, cocking my head at him and smiling. I'm not about to let this man intimidate me. I don't care if he is six foot six at the least.

"Mr. Little, are you dating Tina Glines?" Quentin asks.

"No." Victor looks all too happy to answer that question, so I decide to rephrase it.

"Were you ever dating Tina Glines?"

Instead of answering, Victor looks at Timothy.

"I don't see how that's relevant," the lawyer says.

"Well, considering it gives Mr. Little motive for killing Michael Walberg—*added* motive, I should say since he had motive already after Walberg stole from his gas station." I lace my fingers, mimicking Timothy Little.

"My client's personal life is not up for discussion."

"Oh, but I think it is. You see we have a witness that overheard Tina Glines speaking about your client," I say. "If you prefer to let Tina tell her side of the story, that's fine. We can talk to her." I turn my gaze on Victor. "Of course, if things didn't end amicably between you two, it might be in your best interest to explain things in your own words rather than allow Tina to give us her version of the truth."

"I see what you're doing here, Ms. Coffee," Timothy says. "But it won't work. You're not going to intimidate my client."

"No need," I say. "Tina's quite the talker. I'm sure we'll get what we need from her. And you know, she was in the apartment with the killer. It makes sense why she wasn't harmed. You wouldn't hurt her if you were still in love with her."

Victor sits forward in his seat. "She was there?"

I turn to Quentin to see if he just heard what I did. Is Victor about to confess?

"Victor, don't say another word," Timothy warns him.

"You were in the apartment, weren't you?" I ask.

All the color drains from Victor's face. "I—"

"I insist on having a word with my client. Alone," Timothy says.

Quentin, Cam, and I stand up and exit the room.

"How did you figure that out?" Quentin asks.

"I thought he might get angry and slip up, revealing something we could use."

"Are you saying you don't think he's guilty?" Cam asks.

"I'm saying I don't know. It could be him. Sure. Or it could have been him and Tina. If they were dating, they might have planned this together. I mean it makes more sense for Tina to date a businessman like Little. She told me she wasn't sure why she was with Michael, but maybe that was a lie. Maybe she was with him to help Victor Little get revenge."

"I see what you're saying," Quentin says, rubbing the back of his neck. "And it makes sense that Michael Walberg would open the door for Tina. Victor Little could have come in behind her without Walberg even knowing he was there."

"Did we just solve the case?" Cam asks.

"We need to get back in there and find out," I say.

"Except we all know Timothy Little isn't going to let Victor incriminate himself." Quentin paces the area outside the interrogation room door. "How can we play this to get Victor to slip up again."

"Jo, did pretty well before. Maybe you should let her handle it," Cam says.

Quentin stops pacing and faces me. "Think you can?"

"I'm willing to try. And I have an idea."

A few minutes later, Timothy Little opens the door to tell us we can rejoin them in the room. I have my phone at the ready, pressed to my ear. "Thank you, Tina. You've been very helpful. And yes, Detective Perry will make sure you're protected. He's sending an officer to you now to bring you to a safe location."

"You're talking to Tina?" Victor asks. "She's talking to Tina," he tells his lawyer.

Timothy holds up a hand. "What's going on here?"

"We were getting Tina's statement. Now that she knows we're aware of her relationship with your client, she had a lot more to tell us. It's amazing the deals people will make to get their own prison time reduced." I pocket my phone.

"What deal?" Victor looks horrified. "What did she say?"

"If I were you, I'd start talking, Mr. Little," I tell him. "It's your only chance to make things slightly better for yourself."

"Don't say anything, Victor," Timothy says.

"I knew she saw me. I knew it." Victor leans forward and places his head in his hands on the table.

"You were at Michael's apartment Monday morning," I say.

"Do not admit to that," Timothy says.

"But she saw me." Victor raises his head, his eyes full of tears. "I went to get my money back. But he was dead when I got there."

"Victor, shut up!" Timothy bellows.

"I bent down and my tie got his blood on it. There was so much blood. When I stood up, I felt sick, and I ran for the kitchen sink. I thought I was going to throw up. But instead, my tie dripped blood on the kitchen floor."

"That's when you grabbed the mop to clean it up," I say.

He nods. "Then I realized I was touching things, so I got some rubber gloves from under the sink and I put them on. I cleaned everything I touched with bleach from under the sink, too."

"But Tina arrived."

He nods. "I had the mop in my hand. I ran into the bedroom and hid until she left. Then I returned the mop and snuck out the deck door."

Timothy Little throws his hands in the air.

"She thinks I killed him, doesn't she?" Victor asks me, his eyes red.

"I don't know. I wasn't actually talking to her on the phone."

Victor's eyes widen. "You tricked me."

"I was just going over the conversation I'm planning to have with Tina after we're finished here." I smile at Timothy Little, who is seething, his face as red as a fire truck.

"I didn't kill him. I swear. He was dead when I got there."

"Did you see anyone leaving the apartment complex when you arrived?" I ask.

"Um, there was a car. I think it was dark blue."

"What kind of car?" I ask.

"I don't know. A sedan of some sort."

"Could it have been a Honda Civic?" I ask, and Quentin looks at me. "Grace Clark, the resident who lives below Tyler and Michael drives one." She also said she didn't have classes Monday morning, so why would she have been leaving her apartment so early in the morning?

"I don't know. Maybe it was a Civic. I didn't really pay much attention to it." Victor lets out a deep breath. "I didn't kill him. I know I should have called the cops when I found the body, but since we'd fought in public not long before that, I thought I'd be a suspect."

He thought right. He is a suspect.

"I promise I'll tell you everything I know. I have the video footage of Michael stealing. And I'll give you the metal bar from the door. You can test it for blood. I didn't kill him. I have nothing to hide."

Quentin stands up. "I'll take that metal bar. We'll have it tested for Michael Walberg's blood." He motions for us to follow him out of the interrogation room.

"I think Tina Glines withheld some information from us, and Grace Clark may have lied as well."

"It's late. You two should go home." Quentin looks at his watch, and I can't help wondering what time visiting hours are over at the hospital. I'd feel bad if he missed his opportunity to go see his son.

"Do you want to call us in the morning with the plan?" I ask.

He nods.

Cam drives me back to Cup of Jo so I can get my car.

"How does takeout sound?" he asks me. "I can pick something up and meet you at your place."

"It's like you're reading my mind." I give him a kiss before I get into my car to drive home.

My phone rings on the way, and I answer using my Bluetooth.

"I'm guessing there won't be a big dinner tonight," Mo says.

"No, Cam is grabbing food on his way here. Why? What's up?"

"I wanted to let you know my research into Michael Walberg continues to baffle me. I found a death certificate for another Michael Walberg of the same age who died three years ago. This name is way too common. It's making things really difficult."

"I appreciate you trying, Mo. Go enjoy your evening with Wes."

"I'd tell you to enjoy yours, too, but I know how you get when you're working on a case. It consumes your entire life."

That it does. I hang up with Mo and realize something I haven't questioned before. Why doesn't Michael Walberg have any family looking into his death. Where are they? Why hasn't anyone come to claim the body or make funeral arrangements? He's becoming more of a mystery to me as time goes on.

CHAPTER TEN

In the morning, Quentin has Cam and me meet him at the apartment complex where Tina Glines lives. We need to find out how involved she was with Victor Little and if she knew he was in Michael Walberg's apartment Monday morning at the same time she was.

She's wearing pajamas when she answers the door. "Can I help you?"

"Do you remember us?" I ask her.

"Yeah, you're looking into Michael's murder, right?"

"Yes, and you've met Detective Perry before, too."

She nods. "Come in."

I'm a little surprised she's inviting us in. Her place is neat and nicely furnished. She gestures to the couch, and she turns off the television, which was set to the news.

"I was watching to see if there was any progress on the case. You haven't released much information to the media," she says.

"There's not much to report," Quentin says. "We spoke to your boyfriend yesterday."

Tina looks confused for a moment. Then she says, "Oh. You know about that?"

"Were you seeing both Victor Little and Michael Walberg at the same time, or was the thing with Michael a sham?" I ask.

She narrows her eyes at me. "I'm not sure I understand what you're getting at. Are you accusing me of something?"

"Victor already told us Michael was dead when you arrived at the apartment. He confirmed your story." I look around her place. "What I'm not sure of is why you were dating Michael if you were already with Victor. Victor seems to fit your type much better."

"You don't know me at all, but you think you know my type?" She's much more defensive today than she was yesterday at the nail salon. Maybe it's because we cornered her at work. She might have been putting on a persona so anyone who overheard us would immediately think she'd done nothing wrong.

"You said yourself that you weren't sure why you were with Michael. And now that we know you were also with Victor, I have to concur that you and Michael don't make sense at all."

She inhales deeply, and I have to wonder if it's meant to buy her some time before answering. "Michael had other good qualities." The way she says it makes me hesitant to ask what they were. "Victor has money and good business sense. He's the type of man you keep around. But Michael was fun to hang out with. They fulfilled different needs."

I've heard enough to get what she means. "I see. Did they both know you were seeing other people?"

She nods. "Neither relationship was exclusive."

"So there were no hard feelings between the two men?" Cam asks. I'm sure he can't imagine that. Cam is a "one woman, one man" kind of person. It's another thing I love about him.

"None. Well, that's not exactly true. After Michael stole from Victor, there were plenty of hard feelings. I feel bad that I told Michael about the job opening at the station."

Interesting because earlier she acted like she barely knew where Michael worked. Clearly, she was trying to keep us from finding out how connected she was to all of this.

"You lied to us. What are you trying to hide?" Quentin asks, coming right out with it.

"It's my right not to incriminate myself. I know the law." She crosses her arms and takes a step back to put more distance between us.

"Did you do something you feel you could be incriminated for?" I ask.

"I introduced Michael and Victor. If Victor killed him, I don't want to be seen as an accessory."

Who knew she really would throw Victor under the bus to save herself? I was playing a part at the police station yesterday, but apparently, it fit her personality to a tee.

"Do you think he did kill Michael?" I ask.

She shrugs. "Beats me? I haven't talked to him since. Just to be on the safe side. I blocked his number and everything."

"Then you must think there's a chance he's guilty," Quentin says.

"Yeah, there's a chance."

"Victor was in the apartment with you Monday morning. He says he found the body before you did. He was afraid you'd think he killed Michael, so he hid from you."

She snaps her fingers. "He's a neat freak. I should have known he moved the mop."

"Why would you think he'd go to Michael's apartment?" I ask.

"Because Michael stole money from the register more than once. He was caught in the act the day Victor chased him out, but when Victor went back to review the security tapes, he found out Michael took money the night before, too. I'm guessing he went to Michael's apartment to try to get it back."

"How do you think that conversation would have gone?" Quentin asks.

"Sorry, Detective, but I'm not going to speculate for you. Feel free to ask Victor yourself."

"Why didn't you tell us you were seeing Victor?" I ask.

"Didn't think it was important. Like I said, I didn't know Victor was at Michael's apartment. I didn't see him. I was scared for my own life. You can't blame me for that."

"Is there anything else we should know?" Quentin asks.

"Yeah, like where Michael's family is?" I add. "Why aren't any of them here?"

"I told you he didn't talk about his personal life. I know nothing about his family."

Someone has to know something about this guy. It makes no sense that he's a complete mystery to everyone around him.

"Who was Michael closest to?" I ask.

"I don't want to get Tyler in trouble because he genuinely seems like a nice guy, but he lived with him. He must know some things about him, right?"

Quentin smirks at me, and I know he's thinking he was right about Tyler all along. Seriously, I should sic Mrs. Marlow on him. She'd stand up to Quentin on Tyler's behalf.

"Thank you for your time, Ms. Glines," Quentin says. "If you think of anything else, you have my number."

She gives a curt nod and gestures to the door. She wants us out of her life.

Back at our vehicles, Quentin says, "Grace Clark has classes all morning. We can show up on campus to talk to her between classes, though."

"What is she taking classes for?" Cam asks.

"Business. They're offered at the high school. There's a building in back of the school that's used for continuing education. They used to only offer the classes at night, but this semester they opened daytime courses as well."

"Then I don't think we can just walk on campus, Quentin. High Schools don't really like the general public showing up unannounced like that."

"I'm not the general public," he says. "And since you're with me, it will be fine."

Maybe I should call Erica Daniels to find out for sure. She teaches art at the high school and happens to live in my building. She probably has nothing to do with the continuing education classes, though.

"It's fine, Jo," Quentin says. "This is a police investigation. They have to cooperate with me."

He loves throwing his badge around. No wonder no one in town wants to be near him.

The continuing education building behind the high school has its own entrance, so maybe Quentin was right about it not being the same as trying to get into a high school. The only people taking these classes are adults, and they seem to come and go. There is a man working security as soon as you enter the building, though, and he stops us to see where we're going.

"I see you don't have student ID badges," the man says.

"I have a different badge." Quentin shows him his detective's badge.

"I see. What can I do for you?"

"We need to speak with one of the students here, Grace Clark."

"Oh, I know Grace. She's not here today, though."

"Really?" Quentin cocks his head. "Does she not have a class?" He said he checked her schedule, but I suppose the class could have been canceled.

"She's supposed to, but she didn't show up. It's not like her to miss a class, so I hope she's not sick or something."

I'm rooting for her being sick, because "or something" could be that she's the killer, and she's avoiding her usual routine so we can't find her.

"Thank you for your help," Quentin tells him before turning for the door.

"Do we try her at home?" I ask once we're at our vehicles again.

"Yeah, and she better hope she's there." Quentin slams his car door.

"It's amazing how he can go from thinking Tyler is guilty to blaming everyone we come into contact with on the case," Cam says as we drive to Grace's apartment.

"If by amazing you mean completely idiotic, then yes. It's totally amazing."

Cam laughs. "Be honest. You miss living in a different town than him, don't you?"

I don't miss living in a different town than Cam. Or Mo. Or the rest of Bennett Falls. "I don't miss California." Although, Aunt Cindy and I did have fun together. Dad's sister was happy to take me in for a while so I could get away from Quentin and Samantha. Bennett Falls is home, though. It always will be.

Cam laces his fingers through mine. "I don't miss you living there. I actually thought I was going to have to come get you or resign myself to become a west coast guy."

I laugh. "I love you, but I don't see you wearing surfer shorts."

"Neither do I. I'm really thankful you came home. And who knows? Maybe one of these days, you'll see me wearing a wedding ring."

I turn to look at him. "Is that your way of saying we should pick a wedding date?"

"Subtle, huh? I figure we've decided on everything else, so maybe it's time we pick a date."

We've decided to get married at Cup of Jo and only invite immediate family and friends. It's going to be a very small ceremony. "Honestly, I'd marry you today. The day doesn't matter much to me."

He smiles. "You know, the entire town is going to be mad at us anyway for excluding them, so why don't we pick an evening, get married, and then tell everyone the next day?"

"Do you plan to serve wedding cupcakes to inform everyone?"

"I could."

"Maybe my mom could officiate. That way my dad would give me away, Mo would be maid of honor, and Wes would be the best man. Just the six of us."

He eyes me. "Do you think she would? Because I kind of love that idea."

"Seriously?" I ask.

He nods. "Let's ask your mom if she'll officiate." He pulls up in front of Grace Clark's apartment and parks next to Quentin's patrol car.

"Why do you two look so happy?" Quentin asks. "Did you somehow solve the murder on the way here?"

"Would you really be surprised if we did?" I ask.

He dips his head from side to side. "Not so much. Is that what happened?"

"No. We weren't even talking about the case. We do have lives outside of helping you, you know."

He ignores my comment and knocks on Grace's door.

"Who is it?" she calls from the other side.

"Detective Perry with the BFPD. I need to speak with you."

She opens the door, looking like she hasn't slept in days. Her eyes are puffy, and her complexion is white. "I have to warn you I'm sick, and I have no idea if it's contagious. So you're welcome to come inside, but don't blame me if you get sick. I was throwing up all night."

"Sounds like a stomach bug," Cam says.

"Yeah, some guy in my class yesterday said he was sick all day on Monday. I guess he still wasn't a hundred percent better on Tuesday because here I am, sick as a dog." She cocks her head. "Why do we say that anyway? I've never seen a sick dog."

"Grace, we don't want to keep you. We just have a quick question," I say, getting back on topic. "You said you didn't have a class Monday morning, right?"

"That's right."

"But Michael's music woke you up?"

She nods.

"Did you leave the apartment that morning?"

"Yeah, I figured I was up anyway so I might as well go to the diner and get some breakfast. I love their breakfast sampler that comes with a little bit of everything. I have trouble deciding between pancakes and French toast, so this way I can have both." Talking about food must turn her stomach because she suddenly looks green, and she presses a hand to her mouth. "Excuse me." She turns and runs back into the apartment.

I look at Quentin. "I think she's in the clear. She had no reason to kill Michael. She even seems to have made the most of him waking her up early."

"I guess you're right. And I can't risk getting sick, or I won't be allowed to see Quentin Junior."

"So what now then? What leads do we have?" Cam asks.

"None. We have none," Quentin says.

And as much as I always hate to agree with the man, he's absolutely right.

CHAPTER ELEVEN

Cam and I spend most of the day working at Cup of Jo. I send Jamar home because he tells us Summer is off today. Something about a doctor's appointment she had in the morning and her taking a personal day. He's now spending the rest of the day with her. Robin and Tyler are both here, though.

And Mrs. Marlow has been here all day, watching out for Tyler. I had to switch her over to green tea. I don't want to be responsible for the woman being jittery from drinking coffee all day long.

In the afternoon, I call Quentin to see if he has any updates.

"There was no trace of blood on the metal bar Victor Little threatened Michael Walberg with. We've officially hit a dead end. I hate to say it, Jo, but Tyler is the suspect I haven't cleared yet."

"How can you say that? He was here. He has plenty of witnesses."

"The window for the time of the murder is still unclear. I told you the music Grace Clark heard could easily have been an alarm. Tyler Quinn is not cleared of anything. I'm sorry, but that's just how it is."

Without so much as a word, I end the call.

"You look grumpy," Mo says, walking up to the counter.

"Yeah, well that was Quentin. It's to be expected."

She holds up a hand. "Say no more. I won't argue with you."

"What can I get for you?"

"Actually, I'm here because I was thinking about something."

"What's that?"

"Well, according to Tina, Michael didn't talk about his past, right?"

"Yeah."

"So maybe something really tragic happened to him. He could have been trying to run from his past."

"How does that help us?"

"I think this evening, we should be trying to search his name in connection to some crimes."

"Wait. I thought you meant tragic as in his family was killed in an accident or something. You think he's a criminal?"

"I think he was hiding from someone or something. That doesn't scream accident to me. I think maybe he witnessed something criminal or was involved in something criminal."

I guess it's as good a theory as any. "My place for dinner and research?"

"Is there any other way to spend a Wednesday night?" she asks with an eye roll.

"Not for us it seems." I make her two large coffees and throw in some chocolate sticks and cinnamon buns Cam recently took out of the oven.

"If you keep feeding me like this, I won't fit into my bridesmaid's dress."

I gently tug her arm and lean in to whisper. "We might be tying the knot sooner rather than later."

"What?" she shrieks.

I press a finger to my lips and shush her. "I don't want everyone to hear."

"Sorry, but this is exciting," she says in a loud whisper.

"You might not be that excited when you hear the plan."

"You are not eloping," she says, squeezing my hands.

"Ow, Mo. Let go." I pry my hands from hers. "That hurt."

"Then start talking, and you better hope I like this plan."

Cam walks out of the kitchen and steps between Mo and me. "What's going on?"

"My sister is trying to ruin my life," Mo whines.

"When you get married, you'll be in charge. But this

is my wedding, and I'm doing what Cam and I want. You're going to have to deal with that."

"Tell me these plans I'm going to hate," she grumbles.

"I don't want to now."

Cam shakes his head. "Jo, I love you, but you and Mo have a tendency to revert to your elementary school versions of yourselves when you fight. I'll be in the kitchen if you need me." He kisses my head before walking away.

"He exaggerates," Mo says.

"You're right. We're acting like we're no older than kindergarteners."

"Whatever. This is important."

"Exactly, which is why we should do it the way we want."

She lets out a puff of air. "All right. Tell me."

"We're going to ask Mom if she'll officiate."

"You want her to perform the ceremony?"

I nod. "Think she'll do it?"

"Of course. She's Mom. She'll be honored you asked and probably take the test immediately to get ordained."

"Great. Then Cam and I can pick a date. It's just going to be the six of us. Right here." I wait for her to protest but she smiles.

"You know, it does sound perfect for you guys. Can I pick my own dress?"

"I already said you could."

"I'm just checking. You got mad at me, so I want to

make sure you don't retaliate with the world's ugliest bridesmaid's dress."

"When you put it that way, it's a great idea. I'll pick the dress."

"No! Too late. I'm already eying one up. I'll take a few photos and show you at dinner tonight. What about your dress? Any ideas?"

"Not yet. If you see any while you're getting pictures of yours, let me know."

"I swear you'd be lost without me."

"Keep telling yourself that."

She leaves, yelling goodbye to Cam through the kitchen window.

"Did I hear talk about a wedding?" Robin asks me.

I nearly jump. I hate excluding people. I know I'm going to take a ton of grief for it. Mo was probably right. I should have invited the entire town. But it's not at all what I want. I never envisioned a giant wedding. It's not about the ceremony for me. It's about starting my life with my best friend by my side.

"Hey, don't sweat it. I wasn't expecting an invite. But if you need anything, let me know."

"Actually, maybe you and Jamar should be there."

"Someone's got to serve the coffee, right?" she asks with a smile.

"Would it be wrong to sip coffee between the I dos?"

She laughs. "Not at *your* wedding."

Mo has her phone out as she walks into my apartment. "So not only did I find the perfect dress for me, but I found one for you as well."

Why am I not surprised in the least? "When you say the perfect dress for me, do you mean the dress you think I should wear or the dress I'll love for myself?"

"You tell me." She turns her phone toward me.

The first shock is that it's not white. It's creamier in color. "It looks like—"

"The color of foamy milk on a coffee drink?" She smiles. "Yeah, I'm aware."

The dress is simple but elegant. Nothing over-the-top. But it has a subtle design etched into it. "Mo, I can't believe I'm going to say this, but I think you found my dress."

"I want to see," Cam says, walking over to us from where he and Wes were talking in the kitchen.

Mo grabs her phone from my hand. "No way. Camden Turner, I'm letting a lot slide when it comes to this wedding, but I will not allow you to see her dress before she is walking toward you at the ceremony."

"Mom said yes, by the way," I say to break the tension. "She's getting ordained right away, so when we're ready, she'll be ready, too."

"Great. Then I guess that leaves us to get the dresses altered and the guys to find their tuxes."

"You don't have to wear a tux if you don't want to," I tell Cam.

"I happen to look amazing in a tux."

"I know you do, but you look amazing in everything. You could wear your apron, and I'd still think you were the most gorgeous man alive."

"Gag. Please stop," Mo says.

Wes laughs and wraps an arm around her. "Let them be, Mo. They're happy."

"Where are we on dinner? Is it almost ready?" she asks, changing the subject. It might be the first time she willingly ended a conversation about my wedding.

"Yeah, I just have to take it out of the oven. It's meatloaf and roasted potatoes. Jamar should be here with the wine soon."

"Are we getting away with not eating veggies tonight?" Mo asks, sitting down at the kitchen table.

"You wish. Summer is coming with Jamar. She's making broccoli salad."

"What's that?" Mo asks.

"It's delicious. It has broccoli, almonds, apples, sunflower seeds—"

"Are we late?" Jamar asks.

"No, you're right on time," I tell him.

Summer places the bowl in her hands on the table. "I made a lot because I wasn't sure how many people were coming."

"That looks delicious," Mo says, uncovering the bowl. "I don't think I've ever been so excited to eat my vegetables."

"Glad to hear it. It's one of my favorites. I usually only make it for special occasions."

Cam and I carry the meatloaf and potatoes to the table while Jamar opens the wine and pours everyone a glass. Wes serves the meatloaf, and we all dig in.

All through the meal, we talk about everything and anything but the murder investigation. It's times like this when I feel completely normal and at ease. I can pretend people don't commit horrible acts of violence, and everything is right with the world.

"Word on the street is that Quentin is going to have some competition," Summer says as we're finishing dessert, which is strawberry shortcake and coffee.

"What do you mean?" I ask.

"Well, Jamar and I saw this guy at the park. He was with Chief Harvey. It seemed like the chief was showing the man around town. I heard the chief call him Detective, so I'm assuming he's joining the BFPD."

Probably because Quentin wants to spend more time with his wife and son. "That makes sense."

"Yeah, and maybe you won't get roped into helping with so many cases. This new detective might be better at his job than Quentin is."

"One can only hope," Cam says.

We all talk for a while, and around nine o'clock, Summer and Jamar leave.

"Mo, you never showed me your dress," I say.

"Oh, duh." She pulls out her phone to show me. It's a really pretty coral color, and while the dress is elegant, it still screams Mo.

"It's perfect."

"I'm so glad you said that because I already had the measurements taken and the alterations are underway. I told them to expect you tomorrow for a fitting. They're holding your dress because I put a deposit down. I called Mom from the store, and she insisted on paying for your dress. She said to tell you not to even bother arguing with her because as the officiant, she's in charge."

"Why does everyone think they're in charge of my wedding?" I ask, though I'm touched Mom wants to buy my dress for me.

"Don't worry. The dress was a lot less expensive than I was anticipating. The store has a great sale going on. Plus, the woman who owns the store was a friend of mine from high school, so she's giving me an additional discount."

"Thanks, Mo."

"If that makes you happy, this will really make you love me. I found a few more interesting things about Michael Walberg. Now again, I can't be a hundred percent certain any of the Michael Walbergs I found are actually our victim, but at least this is a start."

"Lay it on me." I lean back on the couch to get comfortable.

Wes and Cam join us from the kitchen. They insisted on doing all the cleanup this evening.

"All right, well, I found an arrest record for a Michael Walberg. It's for theft, which made me think it might be the same guy."

"Based on what we know of the victim, that's a logical assumption to make," Cam says, sitting beside me.

"I thought so," Mo says. "Anyway, this Michael Walberg had charges brought up against him for stealing from a man named Monty Van Buren."

"What did he steal?"

"Van Buren claims Walberg broke into his home and stole money from his wall safe. Apparently, Walberg was employed as the Van Buren's landscaper at the time."

"Sounds like Walberg has had a wide variety of jobs," Cam says.

"Did he serve time for the theft?" I ask.

"No. He fled the authorities. There's a warrant out for his arrest."

"Then if it was the same Michael Walberg, wouldn't the police know about him because of the warrant?" I ask.

"That's what makes this so complicated. The social security numbers are different. They can't link this Michael Walberg to that one, but if you ask me, it has to be the same guy, don't you think?"

"This is weird." I shake my head. "Anything else?"

"Yeah, remember the Michael Walberg who died?"

"Yeah, you mentioned him to me earlier."

"Well, his social security number matches the one belonging to the Michael Walberg who has the warrant out for his arrest."

"Then the real thief is dead," Cam says.

"You don't think it's awfully coincidental that there

are two dead Michael Walberg's who are both thieves?" Mo asks.

"Not if the name is really that common," Wes says.

"Maybe it's a glitch in the system somewhere. It's possible *that* Michael Walberg was mistaken for this one. This one here might be the thief. That would explain why he wouldn't tell anyone about his past," I say.

"Jo's making a lot of sense," Wes says.

"Can we talk to this Monty Van Buren guy and get a description of Michael Walberg?" I ask. "That might put this mystery to bed."

"I'll get a number for him tomorrow." Mo yawns. "I think it's time I get home to my bed."

"Yeah, we have an early meeting at work in the morning," Wes says, standing up and helping Mo to her feet. "Thanks for dinner, Jo."

"You're welcome. Thanks for the research."

"That was all Mo's doing. I take no credit this time."

"See you guys tomorrow," Cam says as we walk them out. "I should go, too," he tells me. "Promise me you'll get some sleep."

"It's not like I can contact Monty Van Buren tonight," I say. "This case is officially on hold until Mo finds me that contact info."

"Good night, Jo," Cam kisses me and raises my left hand between us. "I'm looking forward to the day when saying goodnight means rolling over in our bed instead of me driving home."

"Soon," I say. "Soon."

I close the door for the night after watching Cam walk down the hall to the elevator. My phone rings almost immediately. I grab it off the kitchen counter. "Hello?"

"Jo, it's Quentin. I'm just giving you the heads-up that we're moving forward with Tyler Quinn's charges. I'm putting the case to bed."

"I can't believe you. You're quitting, taking the easy way out. Tyler didn't do this."

"Yeah, well, all the evidence—"

I hang up before he can finish his sentence. I'm not sure how I'm going to get any sleep now.

CHAPTER TWELVE

"You look awful," Mo says Thursday morning.

"Yeah, well, Quentin called me right before bed last night to say he's moving ahead with the case against Tyler."

Mo inhales sharply. "I shouldn't be surprised by that man, but his level of low continues to get lower."

"Sorry for butting in," Robin says, "but does this mean Tyler won't be here today?"

"I'm sure Quentin picked him up from the hotel first thing this morning," I tell her.

"So that's it? The investigation is over?" Robin crosses her arms and leans back against the glass display case.

"In Quentin's eyes maybe, but I'm nowhere near finished."

"Good because I have the number for Monty Van Buren for you," Mo says.

"It's nine in the morning. When did you find time to get that?"

She shrugs. "I couldn't sleep last night, so I did some research."

"You seemed exhausted at my place."

"I was, but once I got home and showered, I got a second wind. Anyway, here's his number." She hands me a piece of paper.

"I should warn you he's really hard of hearing according to what I found online. You're going to need to speak loudly if you want to get any information out of him."

"Maybe we should go see him in person then," I say.

"That would take a long time considering he lives in Phoenix, Arizona now. He moved a few months ago to be closer to his grandkids."

Just my luck. "Okay, thanks, Mo."

"You can thank me with lots of caffeine. I don't think I look as bad as you do this morning, but I probably feel as bad. I do have youth on my side as far as appearances go." She gives me a smirk only a younger sister can pull off.

"Just wait. You're not much younger than I am, and you'll be the big three-oh sooner than you'd think."

She presses a hand to her chest. "Don't curse at me."

"Cursing at you would be telling you I ran out of coffee," I say. The Coffee sisters aren't known for our use of actual curse words. We're much more creative than that. Though a really angry Mo will throw out the term "fart brain." She may only be two years younger than I am, but mentally, she's still a preteen.

I get Mo her coffee, and one for Wes as well. I also pack up some muffins for them. "Here."

"Thank you." She sips her coffee immediately. "Oh, that's the stuff. Any chance I can get a refill in about an hour delivered to my office? I have meetings all day long, and I know I'll need another caffeine boost by then."

"We don't deliver, Mo, and besides, Cam and I might be off trying to clear Tyler's name."

"It's fine. I can run more coffee over to you and Wes," Robin says.

Mo puts a tip in the black and white tip mug next to the register. "That's for Robin. Don't you touch it, Jo."

"Please, she rarely ever lets us give her any money from that mug," Robin says.

That's because a lot of the time, I'm not even here, so that money isn't mine. I'd never take a cut of Jamar and Robin's hard-earned tips.

Mo waves and walks out, and Mrs. Marlow takes the opportunity to approach me. She pulls me aside, and Robin handles the customers who just came in.

"Good morning, Mrs. Marlow."

"Oh, it's anything but. Do you know that no-good ex of yours has Tyler down at the station?"

I nod once. "Quentin told me last night. But don't worry. Cam and I are on this. We'll get Tyler's name cleared." And make Quentin look like an idiot in the process. That will be almost as satisfying as seeing Tyler go free.

"Well, Quentin Perry is a bit shaken up at the moment." Mrs. Marlow is practically shaking herself.

I reach for her arm. "What did you do?"

"I went down to the station the moment Mickey told me the news."

How did Mickey find out when he was at work? It's like he has eyes and ears all over Bennett Falls.

"I told Quentin to release that boy right now, but he refused. He said I should come back here and mind my own business."

Oh boy. You don't say something like that to Mrs. Marlow.

"I reminded him I know every single secret of his. I've known him since the day he was born. I'm not letting any cheating, lowlife cop tell me what to do."

I rub my forehead. "Mrs. Marlow, please tell me you didn't actually say that to Quentin."

"Not those exact words, no." She has the decency to look away, and I know what she said was much worse. "I'd tell you what I did say, but I'm afraid it will make you blush. And there are young children in here." She gestures to a woman balancing her toddler on her hip.

"Oh, Mrs. Marlow."

"He deserved it. Chief Harvey even laughed. Oh, he tried to cover it up with a cough, but I heard it loud and clear. He agrees with me about Quentin."

"Mrs. Marlow, you know I don't like to stick up for

Quentin, but he is going through a lot right now with his son fighting for his life in the hospital. I think we should cut him a little slack by not reducing him to a laughing stock in front of the entire BFPD."

She waves a hand in the air. "That baby is going to be fine. Mickey said he's out of the real danger now. Quentin is cranky because the baby still isn't allowed to come home for a little while longer. And he's married to Samantha. That's enough to make anyone lose their marbles."

I can't argue with her there. "I'm surprised Quentin didn't threaten to arrest you for making a scene."

"Oh, he tried, but I told him what would happen if he came near me with handcuffs."

This time I can't help laughing. "Mrs. Marlow, if I ever find myself in a fight, I want you by my side."

She leans toward me. "I've taken down men much bigger than Quentin Perry."

"I have no doubt that's true. What can I get for you this morning?"

"You can get me some evidence that proves Tyler is innocent. He shouldn't be sitting in a holding cell or an interrogation room."

"I'm working on it."

She takes my hand in hers and covers it with her other. "I know you are. And I also know you and Cam are going to find a way to keep your wedding from being a town spectacle."

My jaw hangs open.

"It's okay. I don't blame you. Just hurry up and marry that man already. I've had my eye on him for years, and I'm not sure I can control myself much longer if he's not off the market." She winks at me.

"I'll keep that in mind."

Jamar walks up behind Mrs. Marlow and spins her around. "There's my favorite lady."

Mrs. Marlow giggles. "You couldn't handle me, Jamar Carter."

"But I can handle your order," he says.

"That I'll allow. Jo has work to do anyway." She smiles at me before following Jamar to the counter.

I take my phone and head to the office in the back. Okay, it's a storage room-office combined, but it works. I dial the number for Monty Van Buren, hoping it's not too early for him to take calls.

"Hello?" he bellows into the phone.

"Hello, Mr. Van Buren?"

"What's that?" he asks.

It must be him. "My name is Joanna Coffee."

"Coffee? I didn't order coffee. Who is this?"

"No, my name is Joanna Coffee."

"Do I want a coffee? Well, I guess. Do you deliver?"

Oh, this is not going to be easy.

"Dad, who are you talking to?" a woman says.

"I'm ordering coffee."

"There's coffee in the kitchen. Give me the phone." There's shuffling on the other end of the line, and then she says, "Hello?"

"Hi, my name is Joanna Coffee."

"Oh. That makes more sense now. How can I help you?"

"Well, I was hoping to talk to Monty about a man who used to work for him."

"I'm afraid my father is very hard of hearing. He doesn't do well with phone calls."

"I hate to bother you, but is there any way you could ask him a few questions for me?"

"What's this about?" She sounds like she's losing patience with me.

"I'm working with the Bennett Falls Police Department. A man by the name of Michael Walberg was murdered."

"You can't possibly think my father had anything to do with it. He left Bennett Falls months ago."

"No, not at all. The man who died used to be employed by your father, and we're trying to find out more about Mr. Walberg. He led a very private life, which makes finding someone who might want him dead very difficult."

"I see. I suppose I could ask him a few questions for you. Hold on." Footsteps tell me she's walking to the kitchen were Monty went to get coffee. "Dad, do you remember someone who worked for you named—" She pauses, waiting for me to repeat the name.

"Michael Walberg, he did some landscaping for your father."

"Michael Walberg? He was a landscaper."

Monty's voice comes booming through the phone. His daughter must be standing very close to make sure he hears her. "I remember him. He stole from me. I caught him in my wall safe."

"Did you hear that?" she asks me.

"Yes. Can he describe what Michael Walberg looked like?"

"Do you remember what he looked like, Dad?"

"I'll never forget his face. He had a crook's face. I don't know how I missed it when I hired him."

That doesn't tell me anything. "Hair color, build?" I ask.

"Can you be more specific, Dad?"

"Pacific? You want to go to the ocean?" he asks her.

"No, describe him."

"Why didn't you say so? He had dark hair and dark eyes. He was shorter than I was but in good shape."

"Dad's tall, six-three. So this man still could have been pretty tall himself," she tells me.

The description fits so many men. "Any distinguishing features?" I ask.

"Was there anything special about him?" she asks her father. "Maybe a tattoo?"

"Yeah, he had a tattoo. It was a symbol. He said it was Chinese. Told me it meant respect." He laughs. "I asked him how he knew that for sure because it looked like a weird drawing of a tribal kind of stick figure. I told him it could have said 'fool,' and the Chinese people would probably laugh at him if they saw it."

Quentin will be able to tell me if Michael Walberg has a tattoo matching that description. "Thank you so much. That was really helpful," I tell the woman.

"I hope you solve the case," she says.

I thank her again and hang up. Then I pull up an image of the Chinese symbol for respect. I see Mr. Van Buren's point. It does look a little bit like a stick figure wearing some sort of headpiece.

I hurry into the kitchen to find Cam mixing some batter at the island. "I need to go to the station. I just got off the phone with Monty Van Buren, and he described a tattoo Michael Walberg had. Quentin will be able to confirm if our Michael Walberg had the same tattoo."

"Since you could easily call Quentin, I'm assuming the trip to the station is also about checking on Tyler."

"Smart and handsome. You really are the full package, Camden Turner."

"I'll go with you. Let me pour this batter into the muffin pan and give Jamar instructions to take over."

In about twenty minutes, Cam and I are walking into the police station. Quentin is seated at his desk doing paperwork, and he doesn't look happy when he sees us.

"If you're here to ream me out, you'll need to get in line."

"I heard Mrs. Marlow let you have it this morning."

"I'm still taking grief about that from the chief."

"She said he got a kick out of it. Did you do something to tick him off?" I ask.

"I don't want to talk about it. And I'm not releasing

Tyler Quinn, so if that's why you're here, you might as well go and not waste either of our time." He juts his chin toward the door.

"I'm not leaving. I came to find out if Michael Walberg has a tattoo."

"Why?"

I sit down across from him, but Cam remains standing. "Because I discovered something strange, and I need to find out if I'm right about this." I pause, but Quentin still doesn't answer my question. "Does he have a tattoo?" I ask.

"Maybe."

"Is it a Chinese symbol?"

Now I have his attention. He raises his head to stare at me. "What is it you think you know?"

"I spoke with a man who Michael Walberg used to work for. He described the tattoo to me."

"That's nice. What does it matter, though?"

"Well, considering the man with that tattoo is supposed to be dead, I found it very interesting."

Quentin shakes his head. "Why? Jo, you aren't making sense. You know Michael Walberg is dead. It's the case I just finished investigating."

"Actually, it's not. You see, the Michael Walberg with that tattoo has a different social security number than your victim."

"My victim has that tattoo."

Bingo. That's what I needed to know. "I had a feeling you'd say that."

He holds up a hand. "Wait. They have the same name and tattoo but different social security numbers?"

"It gets worse. The other Michael Walberg had a warrant out for his arrest, but he's dead, too. He died before your victim."

"Are you saying someone out there is killing off people named Michael Walberg?" Quentin asks.

I didn't even consider that, to be honest. "No. I'm saying it seems odd that two people have the same name, same tattoo, and both were caught stealing."

"Small world. I've seen stranger things, though. So have you." He points his pen at me before going back to his paperwork.

"Quentin, how can you not care about this at all? Your victim has no online footprint. He never talked about his past to anyone, and now we find out he shared a name and tattoo with another deceased man. This is like red flag central, and you're waving your hand at it as if it's all easily explained away."

He sighs and puts down his pen. "Do you think I'm the only Quentin Perry in the world?"

"God, I hope so," I mumble before I can stop myself. Cam chuckles behind me.

"You're not the only Joanna Coffee either. Don't flatter yourself. None of us is unique when it comes to our names. Not unless our parents make up a name completely. There's always going to be someone else out there who shares a lot in common with each of us."

"You show me another Joanna Coffee who owns a

place called Cup of Jo, and I'll entertain that idea for a moment." I lean across his desk. "You can't dismiss this. It's the same man. I don't know how he faked his death and changed his social security number, but he did."

"Are you finished?" Quentin asks.

"No. I want to talk to Tyler."

"Sorry, Jo. I can't allow that."

"Why? Are you afraid I'll rip holes into the case you're making against him? Are you scared I'll one-up you again, but this time on your own turf?"

Chief Harvey steps out of his office and walks over to us. "What's going on here?"

"I was just telling Detective Perry that his victim shares a name and tattoo with another thief named Michael Walberg. Coincidental, don't you think?"

"I'm sure Detective Perry will look into it before he does anything to make this police department look bad," Chief Harvey says, and it's clear that's an order.

"Yes, sir," Quentin says.

"Chief, could I speak with Tyler Quinn? I think he might know more than he realizes."

"Then you admit he's withholding information," Quentin says.

"No. I think he may have overheard something and not know it's important to this case." Tyler lived with Michael. If he overheard a phone conversation, it might have something to do with the person who killed him. "Sometimes witnesses don't even know they have key information in an investigation because it doesn't seem important to them. It only becomes apparent to those with all the details of a case. Wouldn't you agree, Detective Perry?"

Quentin's jaw clenches. "I suppose that's possible."

"Good, then let's go talk to Tyler." I smile and stand up as if the matter is settled. Quentin won't refuse in front of Chief Harvey. He's not going to want to look bad in front of his superior for the second time this morning.

"You can wait in interrogation room one. I'll go get Tyler." Quentin stands up and walks past us. The glare he gives me is subtle, but I notice it. He's not happy with me in the least. I don't care, though.

"Ms. Coffee, Mr. Turner, how is it that you always seem to have information about Detective Perry's cases?" The chief crosses his arms as he studies us.

"Tyler is one of our employees. I guess it was just a stroke of luck for the BFPD that we wound up connected to the victim's roommate."

Chief Harvey lowers his arms. "Luck, you say. Interesting word choice, and I'm not sure Detective Perry would agree."

"Yes, well, he's not my biggest fan either."

"I think he's stuck his neck out on the line for you more than you realize, Ms. Coffee." Chief Harvey turns and walks away, leaving me to wonder what he meant by that. Is it possible Quentin wasn't the one who wanted to arrest me in the past?

CHAPTER THIRTEEN

Tyler is happy to see Cam and me. The poor guy looks like he's been in prison for months, and really, he's only been in a holding cell for a few hours.

"I can't do this, Jo. I'm not cut out for it."

"It's going to be okay, Tyler." I reach across the table and squeeze his hand. "Quentin, can Cam and I have a moment alone with Tyler, please?"

"No. I can't allow that, Jo. The chief will have my head."

After what the chief just told me, I don't push the matter. Maybe I've gotten Quentin in hot water more than I know. I always assumed it was Quentin's feelings for me after our breakup that made him come after me, but what if it wasn't him at all. What if Chief Caswell, the former police chief, was making Quentin point the finger at me? What if I misread the situation because I don't trust Quentin after he cheated on me?

I shake off the thought for the time being because right now I need to focus on the case and get Tyler out of here. "Tyler, you lived with Michael. You must have overheard him on the phone sometimes, right?"

"Yeah."

"Who did he talk to? Besides Tina, I mean. Any family members?"

"I never heard him call anyone Mom or Dad. To be honest, I'm not sure he had any family."

"Brothers or sisters?"

Tyler shrugs. "Not that I'm aware of."

"So you don't know who your roommate talked to?" Quentin asks.

"No. He was really private. He took his phone calls into his bedroom."

"He probably was dealing drugs then," Quentin says.

"You think one of his client's killed him?" Tyler asks.

Quentin gives him a look that's nothing short of "No, I think you killed him."

"Tyler, have you seen Michael's tattoo?" I ask.

"Yeah, it's on his chest. It's a symbol."

"That's right. Well, we found out there's another Michael Walberg with the same tattoo."

"That's weird."

"I thought so, too, especially since this other Michael Walberg died three years ago."

"Why does that matter?" Quentin asks "You said they have different social security numbers, right? That means they aren't the same person."

"How difficult would it be to steal someone else's social security number, especially if they had the same name as you?"

"It scares me that you're asking this," Quentin says.

"I'm not planning on doing it. I'm saying I think that's what your victim did."

"Then both Michael Walbergs would have the same social security number. This doesn't make sense, Jo. You're pulling at straws and confusing yourself in the process."

"There's a warrant out for his arrest. Look into it."

"I'm guessing Mo is the one who discovered this information."

I text Mo, asking for the social security number of the other Michael Walberg. She gets back to me immediately, and I hand my phone to Quentin. "Look it up. I'm telling you it's the same person."

"Fine, I will, but even if you're right, this doesn't tell me who killed him."

"Without knowing who we're actually dealing with, it's tough to figure out who would want him dead."

Quentin stands up. "It figures this case would be such a pain."

"Why this case?" I ask.

"Never mind. I'll look into this." He walks out of the room, and I wonder if he realizes he left us alone with Tyler like we previously requested.

"Tyler, did anyone ever come over to see Michael?"

"Not other than Tina. There was this other girl who

came by once, but she had the wrong guy. She was looking for someone named Theodore. I'm not sure why she thought he lived with me, but when I told her my roommate's name was Michael Walberg she left. I never saw her again, so I guess she found the guy she was looking for."

I turn to Cam. "I think it's time we talk to Tyler's landlord. He must have checked out Michael before allowing him to move in, right?"

"He wasn't on the lease, but yeah, Michael had to meet with Mr. Worthington in person," Tyler says. "I'm guessing he had to give him some personal information as well."

"Do you have a number for Mr. Worthington?" Cam asks.

"It's in my phone, but the detective took that. His name is Jacob Worthington, though. I'm willing to bet he's the only one listed in Bennett Falls."

I can get Mo on it then. I text her, feeling guilty that I'm bothering her again when she said she's swamped with meetings today. "Thanks, Tyler."

Quentin returns. "Okay, so there is a Michael Walberg with a warrant out for his arrest, and there's also a death certificate for him from three years ago. So you're right about that, Jo. But like I said, that doesn't prove anything with this case."

"Where did that Michael Walberg live?"

"Clear across the country."

"Out west?" I ask. "Tina said Michael's stories about

his past contradicted each other. One time he said he lived out west, but later he changed that story. She thought he was lying."

"Michael told me he moved around a lot," Tyler says.

"There you have it, Jo. A lot of people move. I'm not convinced of anything."

At this point, I'm not sure someone coming forward and confessing to the murder would convince Quentin. He's made up his mind that Tyler is the killer.

"Have you run the victim's social security number?" I ask Quentin.

"What for?"

"I'm just curious."

"Well, I don't have time for just curious. I have to—" He stands up again. "I have work to do. It's time for you two to leave and for Tyler to go back to his holding cell."

"Jo?" Tyler says.

"It's going to be okay. We're going to figure this out." I walk around the table and hug Tyler. "I promise."

Quentin ushers us out. "Jo, please. Just let this go."

"Sorry, but I refuse to let an innocent man go to jail for a crime he had nothing to do with. It's clear you're not going to do your job, so it looks like I have to do it for you." I turn on my heel to walk out and see Chief Harvey standing in the doorway of his office. I'm sure he overheard that.

Mo comes into Cup of Jo around three in the afternoon. "Sorry. This is the first break I've had all day. I have fifteen minutes to gulp down some coffee and find Jacob Worthington's address for you."

I motion to an empty table in the corner. "Sit. I'll bring your coffee." I pour an extra-large dark roast and bring it to her.

"Piece of cake."

"You found it already?" I ask, taking a seat.

"Yes, but I meant where's my piece of crumb cake?"

Jamar is spinning a customer nearby and overhears. "I'll get it. Want one boxed up for Wes?" he asks her.

"Please, and another coffee for him as well."

"You got it."

She texts me an address and phone number. "I'm thinking tonight we find all the connections we can between the two Michael Walberg's with the same tattoo."

"I guess that means you and Wes are coming for dinner."

"Yes, and you missed your dress fitting. The bridal shop called me."

I smack my hand to my forehead. "I completely forgot."

"They're letting me take the dress since it's already paid for. You can try it on at your place to see if it needs to be altered."

It would be a miracle if the dress fit as is, but I could really use a miracle right about now. Although, if I could choose the miracle, I pick freeing Tyler over not having to alter my wedding dress.

Jamar comes over to the table with a white pastry box and a coffee. "Here you go."

"Thanks." Mo stands up, placing a tip on the table for Jamar. "Time for me to get back to it. I'll see you later."

"Thanks, Mo," I call after her.

I'd rather talk to Jacob Worthington in person, so I wave Cam over and tell him we have another mission before closing time.

Jacob Worthington lives in a big house not far from my apartment complex. To be honest, I didn't even realize this development existed. It's separated from the road by a line of thick trees, and if you're not looking for the entrance, you'll miss it. Like I have for the thirty years I've lived in this town.

Cam pulls into the driveway and parks behind a black BMW. "Looks like Mr. Worthington does well for himself."

"Very well. I wonder how many properties he manages."

We walk up to the front door, and Cam rings the bell.

A man dressed as if he's going golfing answers the door. "Oh, I thought you were someone else," he says.

"Expecting someone?" I ask.

"Yes, my golf partner for the day." He checks his watch. "I guess she's running late." Meeting my gaze, he says, "Can I help you with something?"

"I hope so. I'm Joanna Coffee, and this is my fiancé, Camden Turner. We were hoping to ask you a few questions about one of your tenants. Michael Walberg."

Mr. Worthington nods. "Are you reporters?"

"No, coffee shop owners, actually."

Mr. Worthington laughs. "Why are you asking about a dead man, then?"

"We do some consulting in our spare time. It seems no one knows anything about Mr. Walberg. Where he's originally from, if he has any family... Things like that. The police don't even know who to contact to come get the body and have it buried. It's sad really." I decide the sympathetic angle is the best one to play.

"That is sad. Mr. Walberg isn't on the lease. When one of my tenants said he needed help making the rent, I agreed to let him interview potential roommates. I insisted on meeting the person before he moved in, of course."

"Did Mr. Walberg give you any personal information?"

"No, he paid me in cash, *when* he paid. He owed me a few months' rent. I threatened to throw him out if he didn't pay. He gave me a sob story about getting fired but told me he had another job lined up and would have my money soon."

Another job? "Did he say where?"

"No, and I didn't ask. I try not to get involved in the personal lives of my tenants. All I care about is getting the rent checks."

"We understand," Cam says.

This is another dead end.

After closing up Cup of Jo for the day, Cam and I head to my place. Mo is waiting in the hallway with two garment bags in her hands. "Don't you think I should have a key for emergencies?" she asks.

"Jamar and I exchanged keys in case of an emergency," I say, moving past her to unlock the door.

"He has a key, and I don't? I'm your sister!"

"Yes, my sister who eats all my food and hates her own apartment. The only time you're in your own place is to sleep and shower. Otherwise you're at Wes's house or here." Wes rents a nice house on Lake View Road. His landlord is getting up there in age, and I suspect he'll sell to Wes in a year or two. I can see him and Mo living there together one day.

I walk into my apartment, and Mo ushers me right to the bedroom. "Come on. Cam and Wes can start on ordering dinner while we try on dresses." She gives them a pointed look before closing us in my bedroom. She unzips the first garment bag. "I think you're going to seriously love this dress. It's even prettier in person."

She's not wrong. I do love it.

"I think it might be a little long for you, but the rest of it is probably going to fit you well." She holds it out to me.

I take it and walk toward the mirror on the back of my door, holding the dress up to my body.

"Rethinking the small wedding because you want people to see you in this."

"No. But I can't wait for Cam to see me in it."

"Well, he's going to have to wait." She turns back to the bed and starts trying on her dress for me to see. I slip out of my work clothes and into the wedding dress. It fits me like a glove. It's a tiny bit long, but with heels, I'll be fine. I walk to my closet and get a pair of black heels. They totally don't go, but I'm just trying to measure the length of the dress. I step in front of the mirror, and Mo stands beside me, looking beautiful in her dress as well.

"If Mom were here, she'd totally be crying right now," Mo says.

"Should we send her a picture so she can get the crying out of the way before the wedding?"

Mo laughs. "Probably." She opens the door a crack. "Hey, Wes, could you come in here please. Not you, Cam. Stay where you are."

"Why does Wes get to see?" Cam protests.

"Because he's not the groom, and I'm not the bride. Don't give me grief, Camden Turner."

I laugh because not another peep comes from Cam.

Wes comes into the room and closes the door behind him. He doesn't even look at me. His eyes are laser locked on Mo. "You look…" His mouth drops open.

"Thank you. We need you to take a picture of us for our mom." She holds her phone out to him. I wouldn't be surprised if I'm somehow not in the frame at all. He's so focused on Mo.

Mo loops her arm through mine, and we both smile. Then she takes the phone from Wes. "Perfect. Mom is going to love it." She pushes Wes from the room. "Out you go. We need to get changed."

"Why do I get the feeling I'm barely going to beat you to the alter?" I ask.

"No. Wes and I haven't been dating nearly long enough to contemplate marriage. We haven't known each other all our lives like you and Cam."

Mo's comment makes me curious about something regarding the case. "Michael Walberg must have had a friend, someone who's known him for years, right?"

"Not everyone does, Jo. What you and Cam have is special. And rare."

"I should have Quentin run Michael's phone records."

"Think he will? I mean he's pretty content to pin this on Tyler."

"If he won't, I'll go over his head to Chief Harvey."

"Huh. If you do that, you might succeed in getting Quentin out of your life for good. He may never talk to you again if you get him in trouble with his boss like that."

My relationship with Quentin is anything but simple. We aren't friends, but we once were. How would I feel if that ended completely? I'm not sure, but I'm not willing to risk Tyler's freedom to keep from finding out.

CHAPTER FOURTEEN

After a delicious takeout dinner from S.C. Tunney's, we all take our coffee to the couch to do some more research.

"I still can't believe Lance delivered food here," Wes says. "You guys have great connections."

"Well, Jo did give Lance a big inheritance check that was meant for her, so I think Lance is pretty willing to do anything for her in return." Mo sips her coffee.

"Plus, Lance is a great guy. He's always willing to help out a friend, and he knows we're working with Quentin on this case. Robin's filled him in."

"I'm still baffled by Robin and Lance dating. I thought Robin and Jamar would end up together," Mo says.

"For one, they're still young, so we have no idea who they'll end up with, but Jamar and Robin tried dating. It didn't exactly go well." I'm relieved, too, because if they did date for a while and broke up, one of them would have undoubtedly quit working at Cup of Jo. I like them both too much to want to risk losing either.

"Mo said you want to look into Michael's phone records to see who he talked to," Wes says. "I might be able to help there."

"How?" I ask.

"Do you really want to know? It's not exactly entirely legal."

He's going to hack into Michael Walberg's phone history.

"Wes, I don't want you doing anything that Quentin can arrest you for later. If I have to go over his head to Chief Harvey for anything, Quentin will be out for blood, and I wouldn't put it past him to go after you to get to me."

"Oh, if he even tried..." Mo doesn't need to finish her statement. We're all well aware that she'd kill Quentin and make sure no one ever found his body. Mo's a little scary at times. Wes is the only person I know of who can calm her down.

He wraps an arm around her and pulls her close to kiss the top of her head. "He'd never pin anything on me. He's not a good enough detective to pull that off."

She smiles and relaxes a bit.

"For now, let's stick to legal activities only, though," I say.

"Way to take all the fun out of the evening, Jo," Mo whines.

"I'd just rather not get married in prison, okay?"

"How do we find out who Michael talked to then?" Mo sighs.

This is a complete long shot, but I call Quentin.

"What, Jo? I'm kind of busy."

That means he's at the hospital visiting his son. I decide to play nice since I need a favor. "Sorry." As soon as the words leave my mouth Cam, Mo, and Wes all turn to look at me like I have six heads. "I was just curious if you knew who Michael communicated with the most. I know he didn't seem to have any family, but maybe we should inform a close friend about Michael's death. He or she might know something about Michael's past and if he does have any living relatives."

"I've already taken care of that, Jo. This case is wrapping up."

"Oh, then you found a family member? That's great."

"She's a distant cousin, but I guess that's better than nothing, right?"

"Yeah, definitely. Is she coming to town to take care of the arrangements for the funeral?'

"There won't be one. She's having Michael cremated."

"She's still coming here, though, right?"

"She's already here. By some stroke of luck, she was visiting a friend nearby, so she's staying in town until she finishes up with the funeral home. Then she'll go back to California."

"I don't suppose you'll give me her name so I can offer my condolences," I say.

"Let it go, Jo. Don't bother this woman just so you can try to get Tyler off the hook. He's not even fighting me on the conviction anymore. He's conceded defeat, and you should, too. Now if you'll excuse me, I need to spend more time with my son."

I'm surprised visiting hours are this late. Before I can protest or even say goodbye, I realize Quentin isn't on the phone anymore. I put my phone on the coffee table and lean forward, resting my elbows on my knees and placing my head in my hands.

Cam rubs my back. "It will be okay."

"How?" I raise my head to look at him. "Quentin said Tyler isn't even fighting the charges anymore."

"Do you think that means he actually killed his roommate?' Wes asks.

"No," Cam and I both say.

"There's no way he did this. He's scared and probably doesn't want to say anything Quentin can twist to use against him." And then there's the other option. Tyler might be so confident I'll save him that he's cooperating with Quentin in the meantime.

Last night turned out to be a bust. I didn't learn anything new other than that Michael Walberg has a distant cousin who lives in California. Quentin told me to stay away from her, but he also told me she's in town and will be going to the funeral home to make the final arrangements for Michael's remains.

I can only guess which funeral home she's going to. We have two in town. One is less expensive, and since everyone thought Michael Walberg had no family to pay for services, I'm assuming that's where I'll find his body. Which means that's where I can run into this cousin of his.

"So you plan to stakeout a funeral home?" Jamar asks me.

"I don't have a better plan. I need to find the cousin and see if she can tell us anything."

"If she's a distant cousin, I doubt she'd know anything." Jamar wipes down the display case with a cleaning rag.

"Normally I'd agree, but Quentin found this woman through Michael's phone records. That means they talked. Even if they were only recently reunited, she could still know something."

"I guess you're right." Jamar shrugs.

Mrs. Marlow walks up to the counter. Her expression is somber. "Any news, Jo?"

I reach for her arm. "Not yet, but I'm doing everything I can. I even have a new lead to follow."

"Did you see the news this morning?" She balls her hand into a fist. "Quentin told the press that the case was closed."

"It's not. He just wants it to be, and Tyler isn't exactly fighting the charges at the moment either."

"He knows you'll save him, Jo. He's a smart boy, and you're a tough cookie. I know you'll set things straight." She turns and walks over to Mickey Baldwin's table without even placing an order.

"I'll take care of things here," Jamar says. "You have enough on your plate."

When did this town start turning to me to solve all their problems?

I look through the window to the kitchen. Cam is still working on getting all the baked goods into the display cases this morning. I don't want to interrupt him. "Jamar, will you tell Cam to meet me at Crenshaw Funeral Home when he's finished up here?"

"Of course, but are you sure you want to go alone?"

"I'm literally going to sit outside the funeral home and wait until I see someone go inside. I'll be fine." It's probably one of the safest things I've done on a case.

"Cam still won't like it." Jamar looks nervous. He and I are close, but he has never hung out with Cam alone. They're friends because of me. Not to mention Cam is one of Jamar's bosses.

"Tell him I didn't give you the chance to stop me. He won't have any trouble believing that."

Jamar smirks. "No, he won't. No one can stop Joanna Coffee when she's on a mission. We're all very much aware of that fact."

I grab my purse from behind the counter. "Wish me luck."

"Good luck, Jo."

"Go get 'em, Jo," Mrs. Marlow says as I pass her table.

I give her a nod and walk out.

Crenshaw Funeral Home isn't open yet for the day, which is what I was hoping for. I want to make sure I don't miss anyone going inside since I have no idea who this cousin is or what she looks like.

It's moments like this that I'm really glad I'm not a police detective. Stakeouts are boring. I should have brought myself some coffee to stay awake, but I was trying to leave in a hurry so Cam wouldn't insist I wait for him. I didn't want to chance missing Michael's cousin, and if she's from out of town, I'm assuming she wants to take care of things here and get home as soon as possible.

After about thirty minutes, which feels more like four hours to me because I'm bored out of my mind, Oliver Crenshaw pulls into the parking lot. I know him from high school. His father used to run this place. In elementary school, Oliver would try to scare kids by telling them stories about all the dead bodies in the funeral home. He even held one of his birthday parties in the funeral home one year. It was a little disturbing. I'm hoping he's matured since then.

I get out of my car and follow Oliver to the front door, which he's unlocking.

"Joanna Coffee," he says when he sees me.

"Hi, Oliver. Long time no see."

"Yeah, it's been what? Like twenty years or something?"

"No offense, but I thankfully haven't had much need to stop by here."

"No offense taken. I understand that people would rather not have to come here." He opens the door and gestures for me to step inside. He flips the light switch for me as well. "What brings you here today?"

"Michael Walberg, actually."

"Ah. There won't be any services. His cousin is having him cremated and taking his ashes back home with her."

I'm glad he's being so forthcoming with this information. I was afraid he'd clam up and refuse to talk to me. It's not like we were ever friends growing up. He used to make fun of my name, and I thought he was the creepy boy who always talked about dead people.

"His cousin is here?" I ask.

"How do you know Michael anyway?" Oliver asks.

"Oh, his roommate works for me."

Oliver bobs his head. "Isn't he the guy who supposedly killed him?"

I roll my eyes and wave a hand in the air with a dramatic flourish. "You know Quentin Perry. The man couldn't catch a killer if the guy was waving a knife in the air and standing under a flashing red sign that said *I did it!*"

Oliver laughs and motions for me to follow him. Luckily, the rooms we pass through are empty, not set up for funerals. "I always wondered how you dated him. You two are nothing alike."

"That's probably the nicest thing you could say to me, so thank you for that."

"I guess we'll call it a momentary lapse in judgement on your part." Oliver brings me into his office. "Have a seat."

"Thank you." I sit in the brown leather chair opposite his desk.

"Tell me why you're really here, Jo," Oliver says, sitting on his desk instead of in his chair.

"Well, Michael spoke very highly of his cousin. I'm assuming it's the one you mentioned. He didn't really talk about any other family, and I wanted to come by in hopes of running into her and offering my condolences."

"That's sweet of you." He cocks his head at me, and I get the feeling he's checking me out.

I stiffen in my chair. "Yeah, well my fiancé, Camden Turner, you remember him, right?"

"That's right. I did hear you got engaged."

"Yeah, deep in wedding plans as we speak. But anyway, Cam was hoping to come see Michael's cousin as well, but since we run Cup of Jo together, he's still there getting prepped for the day."

Oliver stands up and walks around the desk, and I breathe a little easier at the distance it puts between us. "How's Camden doing?"

"Great." I look around. "Do you know when Michael's cousin—I'm sorry. I completely forgot her name. Michael mentioned it, too, but I guess I haven't had enough caffeine yet today." I force a laugh.

"Eliana."

I snap my fingers. "That's it. I don't know how I forgot such a pretty name."

He only smiles in response.

"When is she supposed to come here? Like I said, I'd really like to see her."

Oliver consults his watch. "Soon actually."

"Oh, good. I was hoping I wouldn't have to be away from Cup of Jo for too long."

"Well, you're welcome to stay. I can show you some brochures in the meantime. It's never too early to start planning for your final arrangements."

My jaw nearly drops at that. I'm supposed to be planning my wedding, not my funeral. "Oh, um, sure. I'd love to take some brochures. I'm sure Cam would be interested in that as well." My voice comes out shaky, showing how uncomfortable I really am with the topic.

"Great. Let me go get them for you. I'll be right back." Oliver walks out of the office, but he doesn't get far before I hear, "Camden Turner, how are you?"

I get up and meet Oliver and Cam in the hallway.

"Oliver, nice to see you. I was just coming to meet up with Jo."

"Great. Jo and I were discussing future burial arrangements."

I widen my eyes at Cam, hoping to convey this was not my idea at all.

"Oh, well—" Cam stops talking when the door opens behind him.

A woman walks in. She's young. I'd guess early twenties at most.

"Ms. Walberg," Oliver says, "good morning to you."

Her eyes go to Cam and me. "If you're busy, I can come back."

"No, that won't be necessary at all. As it turns out, Camden and Joanna are here about your cousin as well."

Her eyes widen briefly. "Really?"

"Yes, we wanted to offer our condolences to you," I say. "We know Michael didn't have much family left to speak of."

Her eyes fill with tears. "Would you excuse me for a moment?" she asks, heading toward the bathroom.

"Of course," Oliver tells her. After the bathroom door closes, he turns to Cam and me. "The poor woman. She's been beside herself. It was difficult to even get her to come in. I think she's upset to see her cousin's body. It can be quite traumatizing for some people to see their loved ones after they've passed."

I never understood having an open casket at a funeral for that exact reason. It's not how I'd want to remember a loved one at all, and I often think that must be the first image that pops into a person's head when they think of the ones they've lost.

Oliver gets some brochures to show us while we wait

for Eliana, but after about ten minutes pass, I say, "I'm going to check on her and make sure she's all right."

Cam nods to me.

I open the bathroom door. There are two sinks next to the door and three stalls facing them. Without even stepping more than two feet into the bathroom, I can see all of the stall doors are open.

"Eliana?" I call, pushing each stall door fully open in turn. She's not here. I turn to see the window is open, and the curtain in front of it is blowing slightly in the breeze.

Eliana left through the window. But why?

CHAPTER FIFTEEN

I walk back into the hallway. "Eliana's gone," I say.

"That's impossible," Oliver says, looking up from the brochure in his hand. "She would have had to walk right past us."

I shake my head. "The bathroom window was open."

Oliver's brow furrows. "Why would she climb out the window?"

"Let's check the parking lot for her car," Cam says.

He and I rush outside, but the only cars in the lot belong to us and Oliver Crenshaw.

"I don't understand," Oliver says, standing behind us. "Why would she leave like this? We didn't even finish making arrangements for her cousin."

That's exactly what I want to know.

Back at Cup of Jo, Cam and I sit at a corner table with Mo and Wes, who are taking an early lunch break to help us figure out this case.

"Quentin said this woman, the cousin, will go back to California," I say, gripping my coffee cup with both hands.

"Yeah, we suspected Michael was from the west coast. Tina gave us that tip, remember?" Cam asks.

"Right. I guess that does make sense. But why would Eliana run from the funeral home and go back to California without making arrangements for Michael's body?"

"You said she's young, right?" Mo asks.

I nod.

"Maybe it was too much for her. She might have thought she could handle things, but it was overwhelming."

"I can see that," Wes says. "If she's his only living relative, then all of his belongings and such would be her responsibility now."

"And if he really was dealing drugs and she knew about it, she might have gotten scared and decided it was best to just leave town altogether," Mo adds.

"I guess you're right." I shake my head. "I really hate this case."

"I'll look into her more. Do you know if her last name was Walberg?"

"No, I don't. They were cousins, so it is possible they shared a last name."

"Okay, I'll start there then." Mo sips her coffee before asking, "Have you talked to Tyler?"

"No. I can't bear to go see him. He's expecting me to

fix all of this and free him." My gaze goes to Mrs. Marlow, who is camped out here, most likely so she can find out if there's any news about the case. "I feel like I'm letting Tyler down and Mrs. Marlow, too."

Mo follows my gaze. "She really has taken a liking to Tyler."

Mrs. Marlow's family doesn't live in the area anymore. They all moved away. "I think Tyler reminds her so much of her grandson that she's latched on to him."

"It's sad when people don't have any family nearby."

"Family is sometimes who you choose," Cam says.

I place my hand on his leg. My family has become his over the years since he doesn't have many blood relatives left to speak of.

"Well, Tyler is lucky to have Mrs. Marlow," Mo says.

"Agreed."

"I wish we could have spoken to Eliana," I say. "She might be the only one who knows what Michael was up to that got him killed."

"She might still be in town," Cam says. "Maybe we can call around to the hotels in the area and find out where she's staying."

The Reede Bed and Breakfast was the place to stay for a long time, but after the owner, Mary Ellen Reede got too sick to run the place and a multiple homicide occurred there, Mary Ellen's daughter, Elena, closed the place for good.

"Let's try the Bennett Falls Inn and Suites," Cam says.

"Okay."

"We need to get back to work," Wes says.

Mo stands up, taking the rest of her coffee with her. "See you for dinner later?"

I nod. I haven't given a thought to dinner yet, so we might be ordering pizza or something like that because I'm much more concerned with focusing my attention and time on this case.

Cam and I leave Robin and Jamar to handle Cup of Jo while we go to the Bennett Falls Inn and Suites. The woman at the concierge desk has a stern expression on her face, which doesn't give me much hope of her helping us. She doesn't even look up when we approach.

"Excuse me," Cam says, keeping his voice as friendly as possible.

"Yes?" She continues to type on her computer.

"Hi, we were wondering if you could tell us whether or not a woman by the name of Eliana..." He pauses because we don't actually know Eliana's last name.

"Eliana Walberg," I say, hoping she shares Michael's surname. "Is she staying here?"

"I can't give out information about anyone staying here. Sorry." She still doesn't even look at us.

"You can't even tell us if she's here?" I ask. "We're not asking for a room number or anything."

"Sorry. Hotel policy. My hands are tied."

Cam takes my arm and leads me out of the lobby. "Do you want to sit here and wait?"

"I'm going to try asking Quentin. He's spoken to her, so maybe he knows where she's staying."

We go back to Cam's SUV to watch the entrance and call Quentin.

"Detective Perry," he answers, which means he's either with Chief Harvey and doesn't want the chief to know it's me, or he didn't even look at his phone before answering the call.

"It's me," I say. "Michael's cousin fled the funeral home this morning via the bathroom window."

Quentin sighs. "What did you do?"

"Me? I didn't do anything."

"If she ran away from you, you clearly did. Why don't you just tell me so when she shows up here to ask for a restraining order against you I'm prepared."

Unbelievable! I do his job for him, and he accuses me of harassing a grieving woman. "All I said to her was that I was sorry for her loss. She started crying, went into the bathroom, and never came out. When I went to check on her, I found the window open and the bathroom empty."

"When I spoke to her, I asked about Michael's activities," Quentin says. "When I said he was a suspected drug dealer, she got very on edge. My guess is she wanted to get away from any trouble he was in as soon as possible. She doesn't know you, and you showing up to offer condolences probably struck her as suspicious."

"So you're blaming me?"

"No, I'm saying you spooked her. I didn't say you tried to."

I'm not sure it's any different since the outcome was the same. "Do you plan to follow up with her?"

"About what? I put her in contact with the funeral home. That's really where it ends. Now, I have other work to do, so if you don't mind—"

"Where is she staying?" I ask before he can hang up on me again.

"You know I can't tell you that. The woman already ran away from you once. If you hunt her down again for no reason, she will be able to get a restraining order against you for harassment. Is that what you want?"

I'm too angry to respond to that.

"It's over, Jo. I'm sorry. I know you like Tyler, but he's guilty. Maybe it was an accident. Maybe he didn't mean to kill Michael, but he did."

"I refuse to believe that." I end the call, dropping my phone into my lap and leaning my head back against the seat.

Cam rubs my leg. "We'll figure this out, Jo."

"Are you sure about that? Because I have no answers. If this was a drug deal gone bad, the killer is long gone. Tyler will go to prison for a crime he didn't commit."

"Quentin will never get the charges against Tyler to stick. There's no murder weapon or concrete evidence against him."

"He'll still have to endure a trial. And the killer is going to get away with it."

"I'm not sure there's anything we can do about that now."

We spend the rest of the day watching the Bennett Falls Inn and Suites, but either Eliana was never staying here or she's already gone back to California. We order a few calzones and garlic knots for dinner because I'm too angry to cook.

Midnight spends the evening with us curled up on my lap. She seems to know I'm in a bad mood, and she purrs against me. I stroke the top of her head.

Mo is on her laptop next to me on the couch. She's been silent for a long time, which means her search isn't going well. Cam and I have talked through everything we know about the case, and it hasn't helped at all.

"For once I see why Quentin hasn't solved the case," Wes says. "This is a tough one for sure."

"We know Tina Glines wasn't in love with Michael and was dating his former employer from the gas station. She could have only started seeing Michael to help Victor Little get back at him for stealing from the gas station." This is the third time I'm saying this tonight, and it still doesn't sound like a reason to kill someone.

"Or Jacob Worthington, the landlord, might have gone to collect the missed rent and gotten into an altercation with Michael," Cam says.

I shake my head. "I think he'd just evict him, though. Get a new tenant and sue Michael in the meantime. Murder is too extreme."

"Monty Van Buren doesn't even live here anymore,

and he's too old to seek retaliation for Michael stealing from his wall safe when Michael worked as his landscaper," Cam says.

"Jo, I think I found something really disturbing," Mo says.

"What?" I turn to face her.

"Eliana Walberg is related to the other Michael Walberg, not this one." She turns her laptop to me, and I see a photograph of her with a man that is definitely not our victim. He's tagged as Michael Walberg.

"Then why is she here?" It's not like Michael's body was beaten beyond recognition. She would know in a heartbeat that he wasn't her cousin. Not to mention the other Michael Walberg died three years ago. If she got a call from the authorities saying her cousin died, she'd tell them they had the wrong person because her cousin was already dead. This doesn't make sense at all.

"I don't know." Mo scrolls through the site. "Wait. That Michael was her brother, not her cousin."

"Her brother?" Wes asks.

Mo nods. "Yeah. Here they are with their parents."

"Then why was she in contact with this Michael Walberg?" Cam asks. "Quentin located her from Michael's phone records. They were talking."

"I hate to suggest this, but maybe you should bring this information to Quentin. Something is wrong here." Mo gives a small shrug.

"She's right, Jo. We have to go to Quentin. Eliana is clearly lying about her involvement with the victim."

That would explain why she ran from us. "If she thought we were friends with Michael, she might have suspected we knew she wasn't really his cousin," I say.

Cam nods. "And that's why she went out the bathroom window at the funeral home."

"Mo, did you find out anything else about Eliana Walberg?" I ask.

"Just that she's lived in California all her life, and her older brother, Michael, died three years ago. He was assaulted with his own golf club."

"Where?" I ask.

"At the country club he belonged to. I guess he was taking a shower after playing a round of golf, and someone attacked him." She squints at the screen. "I'm reading the article about his death right now."

That means someone was waiting for him. Someone who knew Michael Walberg was there playing golf and would shower before leaving the club. I bite my lower lip as I think.

"Maybe it was someone he played golf with that day," Wes says.

"Killing someone because they beat you in golf seems a bit extreme," Mo says.

"As if we haven't seen people kill for less." Wes shakes his head. "People do really insane things when they're angry."

"Plus, if they belong to a country club, they probably have money. Maybe they made a bet, and the killer lost a lot of money because of it."

Money is a big motive in murder. "I'm more inclined to believe that's what happened. But how do we find out who *that* Michael Walberg played golf with that day?" I ask.

"Why do you want to know?" Mo says. "That's not the murder we're trying to solve."

"Was it ever solved?" I ask her.

"Are you going back to the theory that someone is killing people named Michael Walberg?" Cam asks. "Because I have to admit that seems farfetched to me."

Mo chuckles, which makes us all look at her. "Sorry, but I had a thought. It's not funny, funny, but more like ironic funny."

"What is it?" I ask.

"Well, I was just thinking. Tyler's roommate and this other Michael Walberg were both thieves, right?"

"They both had records for stealing, so yeah, I guess so," I say.

"Well, what if the other Michael, the one in California, stole someone's identity and that's how he got into the country club? Maybe he wasn't really the club member, and he hustled some guys in golf."

"You think they found out and killed him for it?" I ask.

She looks down at her lap. "It's probably a dumb theory. I'm tired, so my brain is grasping at straws."

"It's late," Wes says. "We might be able to come up with something better in the morning after we've all had some solid sleep."

After saying goodbye to Mo and Wes, Cam turns to me. "Are you going to be okay?"

"Yeah." I hold up Midnight, who is snuggling against my chest. "I'm in good hands."

Cam kisses me goodbye. "Try not to stay up too late. You need sleep."

I nod in agreement that I do need sleep. The problem is I have no intention of getting any. I need to find out everything I possibly can about both Michael Walbergs because there has to be a reason Eliana Walberg was talking to the victim, and I have a feeling when I figure out what that reason was, I'll find the killer.

CHAPTER SIXTEEN

"I see you didn't take my advice," Cam says when I drag myself into Cup of Jo Saturday morning.

"Eliana and Michael Walberg are from a wealthy family. Michael was a beloved member of the community."

"Okay." Cam walks toward me and wraps his arms around me. "Why is that important?"

"Because there was a warrant out for Michael's arrest. Why would he steal if he had a lot of money?"

"Maybe out of boredom or for the thrill of it." Cam pulls away. "Who knows?"

"Something isn't right about this. Eliana's brother was in the top five of his graduating class. He went to college on a golf scholarship. He was going to be a doctor. Does that sound like someone who would turn to thievery to you?"

"No, it doesn't. Do you think maybe the arrest

warrant was for a different Michael Walberg? If there really are so many people with that name, it's possible their social security numbers got mixed up. Maybe it was Tyler's roommate after all. Eliana might have been talking to him to try to get that cleared up so her deceased brother wouldn't be tied to illegal activity."

"You mean like she was trying to clear his name and restore his reputation?" I ask.

"It would make sense."

I nod. "Maybe I should ask Tyler about her. It's possible he heard Michael mention her name."

"Maybe. Do you think Quentin will let you in to see him, though?"

I shrug. "If I go to the station now, I might beat Quentin there."

Cam turns back to the oven. "I'm not ready to leave yet."

I squeeze his arm. "You stay. I can handle this. I'll only be talking to Tyler. I won't be in any danger at all."

Cam nods. "Okay. I guess you're right." He kisses me. "Hurry back."

"I will."

I drive to the police station. With any luck, Quentin went to the hospital to see his son before heading to work.

The station is pretty empty. Chief Harvey's office door is closed, and the lights are off. Officer Liberman is at his desk, so I walk over to him.

"Good morning, Officer Liberman. I was hoping to have a word with Tyler Quinn."

"The guy Detective Perry has in holding?" he asks me.

I nod. Officer Liberman is about my age and new to the force, but he's well aware that I help Quentin on cases. "Yes, I need to check something with him. It will only take a minute."

"I should call Detective Perry first to make sure it's okay." Officer Liberman reaches for the phone on his desk.

"He's at the hospital visiting his son," I say. "His phone won't be on."

"Oh." He puts his hand down. "I guess if it's only for a minute, it will be okay."

"Thank you. I'm trying to help Detective Perry as much as possible given his current situation."

"Yeah, I still can't believe it myself," Officer Liberman says. "The man practically lived and breathed this job, but now with his son..." He stands up and shakes his head. "It's a tough situation."

"It is."

Officer Liberman brings me downstairs to where Tyler is. "I can't let him out of there. You understand, right?"

"Of course. Thank you."

He gives me a curt nod and walks back upstairs. Apparently, I'm trusted alone with a jailed suspect. Or at least in Officer Liberman's eyes.

"Hi, Tyler," I say.

He's sitting on the small cot, not looking at me. "It's okay, Jo. I'm sure you did your best. Mrs. Marlow told me how many cases you've solved, but even the police get stumped, so I didn't expect you to pull off a miracle for me."

I step toward the bars. "I'm not giving up yet, Tyler. I'm here to ask if you ever heard Michael talking to anyone named Eliana."

Tyler raises his gaze to mine. "I never heard him use the name, but the woman who came to the apartment, the one looking for Theodore, her name was Eliana."

Eliana is definitely hiding something. She knew Michael. It could be that she was trying to clear her brother's name for something this Michael did. But why did she run? Did she find the body first, and she's worried she'd get blamed if the police found out?

"What did she say to you?" I ask.

"She said she was looking for Theodore."

"Did she give you a last name for Theodore."

Tyler rubs his forehead. "Yeah. It was some type of pattern."

"Pattern? Yeah, I think there's a country singer with the same last name, too."

I don't listen to country music, so I'm not sure what he's talking about. "A pattern like stripes or polka dots."

"Yes, but neither of those."

"Checkers?"

"No."

"Plaid?"

"No, but it did start with a P."

I think for a moment. "Paisley?"

He snaps his fingers. "That's it. Theodore Paisley."

I grab my phone from my purse and text Mo, asking her to find out everything she can about Theodore Paisley. "Why would Eliana think that Theodore, not Michael, lived with you instead?" She had to be calling Michael about the name mix-up. It's the only reason for her to travel across the country to see him.

"I don't know."

"What else did she say?"

"Um…" He lets out a deep breath. "I told her no one named Theodore lived in the apartment and that it was just me and Michael."

"How did she react to that?" I ask.

"She seemed really surprised. She repeated it back to me and asked me Michael's last name."

"But she knew Michael's last name. He had the exact same name as her brother. And Eliana had been calling Michael because of a mix-up with their social security numbers."

"Wait. What? Are you serious?"

"Yeah. Did Michael mention anything about that to you?"

"He said he couldn't get a bank account or anything because of some problem with his social security number. He only ever used cash."

So maybe the mix-up was causing problems for him, too. But who is Theodore Paisley?

"Tyler, I have work to do. You sit tight. I'm going to figure this out."

He stands up and walks to the bars, placing his hands on them. "It's really okay if you don't, Jo. I appreciate you trying."

"Why are you acting like you're giving up?"

He shrugs. "I can't afford a lawyer. They'll appoint some public defender to me who probably won't care about me or my innocence in the least, but what can I do about it? There are things in this world that we just can't fight."

"Yeah, well, call me stubborn or stupid or whatever else, but I will fight Quentin Perry on this conviction. I can assure you of that."

I say goodbye to Tyler and walk back upstairs, but before I turn the corner, I hear Quentin and Chief Harvey talking.

"I don't know why she's here, but she has nothing to do with this," Quentin says. "She barely even knows the guy. She hired him a week ago. I'm one hundred percent positive she doesn't have any information."

"She's made this department and specifically you look bad time after time," Chief Harvey says.

"Only because she's good at solving mysteries. Maybe you should hire her as a consultant. You'd be better off. She's smart."

"She's nosey. She gets involved in things she has no

right to. Tell me how I'll justify hiring a coffee lady as my top consultant. The media would have a field day with it."

"No worse than they do when Jo solves a case before us." Quentin's voice is different. Usually, when he talks to the Chief, his tone is much more submissive, like he's afraid of losing his job. But there's none of that now.

"Watch yourself, Perry. I know the story about you and Jo. I get that you think you owe her something for your indiscretions, but I won't let you make that my problem. Do you understand me?"

"Yes, sir."

The chief's footsteps sound across the floor, and Quentin turns the corner, walking right into me.

"Sorry," I say.

"You shouldn't be here."

"I thought the chief was starting to come around to me. I guess I was wrong."

"You heard that?" Quentin looks more nervous than angry that I was eavesdropping.

"Some of it. It's true then. You've been sticking your neck out on the line for me. Why then did you let me think you were the one always trying to accuse me of things?"

He cocks his head at me. "I'd never throw my chief under the bus."

Since I moved back to Bennett Falls, Quentin's worked under two different chiefs. I guess I annoyed both pretty equally.

"Chief Harvey takes it out on you, doesn't he? The things I do, I mean."

"It's no big deal. Why are you here, though, Jo?"

"I found out something. Eliana Walberg went to see Michael Walberg, I thought it was to clear up the social security mistake that involved her deceased brother and the victim. But when she got to the apartment, she asked for Theodore Paisley, not Michael Walberg."

Quentin looks over his shoulder. "Look. I need to you to leave the station. Can we meet at your place?"

"My place? Why?"

"Because I don't want anyone here to know I'm working with you. But I have an idea, and we might need your sister."

"Okay, I'll meet you at my place in ten minutes," I tell him.

"Hey, do me a favor and look annoyed with me when you walk out of here." He wants everyone to think we fought.

"I have plenty of experience with that emotion when it comes to you, so I have no doubt I can pull it off."

He smirks but quickly makes his expression neutral again.

I take a deep breath and push past him, letting out a frustrated groan as I pass Chief Harvey's office. He looks up from his desk, but I keep my jaw tense and keep walking right out of the station.

I call Mo from the car.

"Hey, so I'm searching that name."

"Where are you?" I ask.

"Wes's place. We're getting ready to go meet a few of his friends from out of town. Why? Please don't say you need me for anything other than looking up this Theo person."

"No, go have fun. I'll deal with Quentin myself. One of us should enjoy our Saturday."

"Okay, well, Theodore Paisley lived in California until about three years ago."

"Three years ago? That's when Michael Walberg, Eliana's brother, died."

"Yeah, about that. Remember how we found out that Michael Walberg was beaten to death with his own golf club?"

"Yeah." I don't think I like where this is going. I inhale sharply. "Go on."

"Theodore used to work at the country club Michael Walberg belonged to. The one where he was murdered."

"Did they have a history? Any mention of them not getting along?"

"I can't find that sort of stuff online, Jo, but Theodore was fired for dealing drugs at the country club. Guess who reported him."

"Michael Walberg," I say.

"You got it."

"Theodore has a warrant out for his arrest, but he dropped off the face of the earth. There's no record of him after Michael Walberg died."

And I know why. "Theodore ceased to exist when Michael died."

"What do you mean?"

"I mean Theodore killed Michael and then he stole Michael's identity. That's why Eliana came here thinking she was going to find Theodore Paisley. Except Tyler told her his roommate's name was Michael Walberg."

Mo gasps. "You don't think—"

"That Eliana avenged her brother's death? Yeah, that's exactly what I think."

CHAPTER SEVENTEEN

I get off the phone with Mo and dial Quentin. "Change of plans," I say the second he answers. "I know who killed Michael Walberg."

"Where are you?" he asks.

"On the road. But we need to find out where Eliana Walberg is staying." If she's even still in town. "And we need to go see her immediately."

"Is she in danger?" he asks.

"No, she's your killer. I'll explain everything, but I need you to find her. Cam and I checked the Bennett Falls Inn and Suites, but we couldn't get any information out of the concierge, and we didn't see Eliana when we staked out the place."

"Someone who wants to lay low would check into the motel on Eighth Street," he says.

"I'll meet you there."

"Jo, I need to know what's going on. Don't you dare hang up on me."

I turn my car around to head to the motel. "Okay, so Theodore Paisley is your victim. He stole Michael Walberg's identity. And after the real Michael died, I think Theodore managed to change his social security number to that of a different Michael Walberg."

"Why did Paisley kill Walberg if he wanted his identity?"

"Anger. Walberg got Paisley fired for selling drugs at the country club in California. Paisley decided to get revenge. I'm willing to bet he emptied as much of Walberg's bank accounts as he could before he killed him. Tyler said his roommate was living on cash alone. He didn't have credit cards or a bank account."

"All right. So he killed Walberg and moved across the country. Why keep his name?"

"Probably to avoid suspicion. Eliana clearly suspected Paisley, but it took her three years to track him down." Another thought hits me. "She didn't know that's who she was contacting at first. She probably tried to track down every Michael Walberg she could find in order to fix the mess-up with her brother's social security number. Paisley got into all sorts of trouble, stealing from multiple people, and he did it with Eliana's brother's social security number tied to his name. That's how she found him."

"She must have hired a private investigator," Quentin says.

"Probably. He tracked down your victim and got his number for Eliana, but she must have recognized Paisley's voice. They spoke on the phone."

"Theodore Paisley could have easily lied and said the number used to belong to a Michael Walberg before it became his. That happens all the time with cell phone numbers. He easily could have played that off."

"And Eliana played along pretending not to suspect he was really Theodore Paisley."

"You think she came here to get revenge."

"I don't know if she intended to kill him. Maybe she just wanted to confront him or report him to the police, but when Tyler told Eliana that his roommate's name was Michael Walberg, she thought Paisley was still trying to pass himself off as her brother."

"Which most likely enraged her further," Quentin says. "Jo, you did it. You figured it all out. Again."

"We have to find her. That's the only way to know if I'm right."

We pull into the motel parking lot at the same time. One car in the lot strikes my eye. A blue sedan. The same one Victor Little, Paisley's former employer at the gas station, said he saw in the parking lot of Paisley's apartment before he found him dead.

I get out of my car and point to the sedan. "Are you thinking what I'm thinking?" I ask Quentin.

"That Eliana Walberg was still in the parking lot of Tyler and Theodore's apartment when Victor Little showed up the morning of the murder?" he asks me and immediately bobs his head. He grabs his gun from the holster on his hip. "Stay behind me at all times, Jo."

"All she's armed with is her brother's golf club," I say.

His eyes widen at me. "The murder weapon. It wasn't a broom. It was a golf club just like Paisley killed Michael Walberg with." He shakes his head.

"I bet it's in there with her or in her car, but I'm more inclined to think she keeps it on her."

The car is parked in front of the door with a big number four on it, so Quentin and I walk up to that one. He knocks on the door. "Eliana Walberg, this is the Bennett Falls Police. Open up."

There goes the element of surprise now that he just announced us.

Something clatters to the floor inside the motel room.

"She's in there," I say.

"I can't just barge in. We have no proof yet. We're only speculating."

"She can't get out any other way than this door, right?"

"There's probably a window in the back," Quentin says.

I know how much Eliana loves escaping through windows. I run around the side of the building.

"Jo!" Quentin yells.

Eliana has one leg out the window when I turn the corner.

"Eliana, stop!" I yell, more to alert Quentin that she's

getting away than to get Eliana to slow down at all. "I know why you did it!"

She scrambles the rest of the way out the window and drops to the ground. She's gripping the golf club in her hand. "Stay back! I will use this."

"I know you will, but only if you're forced to, right? That's why you killed Theodore Paisley. He left you no choice. He took your brother's life and ruined his good name in the process."

"My brother was a good man." She shakes the golf club at me, gripping it tightly with both hands. "He was only twenty-four when Paisley killed him. He stole all his money first. He took everything my brother had, and then he ended his life. And why? Because my brother turned him in for selling drugs. Paisley was a criminal, and he tried to make everyone think my brother was a thief. But he wasn't. He never did anything illegal."

Quentin steps out from around the corner, his gun raised. "Don't move!"

I hold up a hand to him. "Eliana, why didn't you go to the police?"

"Why would they believe me? Paisley is a liar. He somehow managed to steal social security numbers, identities, you name it. I couldn't risk him getting away with it."

"But killing him doesn't make him pay for his crimes," I say.

"He got what he deserved." She sniffles.

I step toward her. "Eliana, put down the golf club. Michael wouldn't want you to do this."

"You didn't know him, and you don't know me."

"Put down the weapon," Quentin says.

"No. I'm not letting you lock me up."

"An innocent man is behind bars right now for a crime you committed," I say. "How is that fair. You're taking his life from him, just like Theodore did with your brother."

"No, it's nothing like that. You know he didn't do it. You won't convict him now."

"I wouldn't, but come on Eliana. You know how the law is. The police will make sure someone pays for this crime, and if they can't bring you in, they'll blame Theodore's roommate."

"He's probably no better than Paisley if they were roommates."

"You're wrong. Tyler is a sweet kid. One of the nicest people I've ever met. You met him. I'm sure he was really nice to you, too."

She waves the golf club in the air. "I'm not coming with you. You'll have to shoot me."

"I really don't want to do that," Quentin says. "Just put the weapon down, and we can talk."

"Talk? You think that will bring my brother back?"

"No, but you can restore your brother's reputation," I say. "You know the truth. Detective Perry will let you tell it."

"What does telling him do?" Eliana asks, shaking her head. "No, it's not good enough."

"He can have you tell your story to the press. They'll get the word out about Paisley and what really happened. I promise you."

"Eliana, this is your one chance. If you resist arrest and I have to shoot you, your story will die with you. Your brother's memory will remain tarnished forever," Quentin tells her.

Her mouth drops open.

"Worse, the rumors about your brother will probably intensify if Detective Perry has to shoot you. Your whole family will be disgraced. Is that really what you want?" I ask.

She grits her teeth and screams as she swings the golf club at me. It flies out of her hands. I duck, and Quentin has to dodge the flying object as well. Eliana takes off running into the woods behind the motel.

I chase after her. "Eliana, stop!" I know it's stupid to try to catch her myself, but she's unarmed. At least it will be a fair fight.

Quentin curses behind me. "Get down, Jo, so I can get a clear shot."

I don't listen. "I'm not letting you shoot her."

Eliana jumps over a fallen tree branch. I try a different tactic. I step up onto the branch and throw my weight forward. I just barely manage to grab her shirt and bring her to the ground with me.

"Get off me!" she screams as she tries to swing her

arm behind her back at me. I have her pinned to the ground, though.

Quentin holsters his gun and cuffs her hands before helping me to my feet. "You couldn't even let me take her down, could you?"

I smirk. "What can I say? I was always a faster runner than you."

He rolls his eyes as he gets Eliana to her feet. "I'd say this case is closed. We have a confession and a murder weapon."

"Then let's go free Tyler. I want my employee back."

EPILOGUE

Tyler is back at work Sunday morning. Robin and Jamar both have the day off. Finally! I thought Tyler might need some time to recover from his ordeal, but he was eager to get back to life as usual. He's also going to find a new apartment. I can't blame him for not wanting to live where his roommate was bludgeoned to death with a golf club.

Eliana Walberg confessed to Theodore Paisley's murder, and Quentin contacted the police in the town where her brother was killed so they can finally put that cold case to rest as well. According to Quentin, Eliana is at peace now. I'm not sure she'll feel that way when she's serving jail time, but she'll have the rest of her life to come to terms with her actions.

Mrs. Marlow walks up to the counter and gives me a hug. "I knew you'd do it, Jo. I just knew it."

"Mrs. Marlow, Tyler is really lucky to have you in his life."

"I was thinking about that. I know he's looking for a new apartment, and my house is too big for one person."

"Seriously?" Tyler says, coming up behind her. "You'd rent me a room?"

"More than a room. My bedroom is on the ground floor. I don't even use the upstairs anymore. You could have it converted into a full apartment, or we could share the whole house. Whichever you prefer is fine with me."

Tyler reaches out and hugs her. "You really are the best. I don't know how I lucked out like this working for Jo and Cam and meeting you." His eyes fill with tears.

"You're one of us now," Mrs. Marlow says, hugging him back. "We take care of our own."

"That's very true," I say.

Cam comes out of the kitchen as Tyler and Mrs. Marlow walk back to her table. "Did I hear he's moving in with her?"

"Yeah. Isn't it great? She'll have someone there if she needs help, and he'll have a pseudo grandmother to look out for him."

Cam wraps an arm around my waist and whispers in my ear, "Speaking of having someone there all the time, I think we need to pick a date to get married so we can be there for each other all the time, too."

"I couldn't agree more." I turn my face and kiss him.

The sound of someone clearing their throat gets my

attention. "Quentin, what brings you here?" I say, turning to face him.

"Do you have a minute?" His tone is somber, and I'm worried he's going to tell me something is wrong with his son.

"Yeah."

"Go," Tyler says, coming back to the counter now that Mrs. Marlow is seated. "I'll take care of the customers."

"I'll get us drinks," I tell Quentin.

Cam nods to Quentin, but Quentin extends his hand.

"Cam, I've learned two things recently, although I probably should have figured them out a long time ago. First, Jo is better than I am at just about everything." Quentin chuckles.

"I won't argue with that," Cam says, shaking Quentin's hand.

"Second, you two are perfect for each other, and I'm really happy for you both."

"Thank you," Cam says, and Quentin goes to find a table. "Was it just me, or was that odd?" Cam asks me.

"It was a little strange," I admit.

Cam kisses the side of my head before returning to the kitchen.

I finish making the Viennas and bring them to the corner table where Quentin is seated. "What's going on?" I slide one drink across the table to him.

"Things aren't working out the way I'd hoped."

"Is Quentin Junior—"

"He'll be okay. But I need to devote more time to being home with him and Sam, and I can't do that in Bennett Falls."

My mouth drops open. I can't be hearing him correctly. "You're moving?"

He nods. "Samantha's parents just bought a big plot of land. There are two houses on it. It used to be a farm, but the farm itself has been vacated for years. It's close to a police academy."

"Wait, you're going to teach?" I ask.

He nods. "It's safer, and I'll be able to spend more time with Sam and Quentin."

"Is that what you want? Won't you miss being in the field, solving cases?" That was the reason he turned down the position as police chief.

"I'm sure I will for a while, but I think over time I'll grow to like teaching."

I let out a small laugh. "You used to teach me every-thing you learned. That's what started my interest in these cases."

"If I'm being honest, telling you all about my own training was a way for me to study."

"I know." Quentin always did what was best for him when we dated. It's strange to see how different he is with Samantha and Quentin Jr. They're his focus now, and I think that's good for him.

"I'm sorry, Jo. I know I hurt you, and I'll never forgive myself for that. You were a good friend. And you're a good detective, too."

This is sounding more and more like a goodbye, and after overhearing Quentin's conversation with Cam a few minutes ago, I realize that's exactly what this visit is. A goodbye. "When are you leaving?"

"The hospital is transferring Quentin Junior in less than a week. I turned in my resignation thirty days ago. Today was my last day. I told the chief I wanted to close this case before I left, and now I'll be moving us into the new house so it's ready when Quentin can come home."

Little things the chief and Officer Liberman said to me now make more sense. They knew Quentin was leaving the BFPD.

"Quentin Junior's really doing well?" I ask.

Quentin smiles. "He's doing great. We got lucky."

I have a feeling this move is to make sure Quentin Junior gets the best care and the best possible life his parents can give him. Samantha can barely take care of herself, but living on the same property as her parents and having Quentin home more will mean the baby will be in good hands all the time. "I'm happy for you guys."

Instead of looking happy, Quentin frowns. "I'm worried about you, Jo. With me gone, you can't get yourself involved in any more murder investigations. You won't have anyone to have your back."

Now that I know Chief Harvey has it out for me and Quentin's actually been protecting me, I'll be more careful.

"Yes, she will," Cam says, sitting down beside me. "She'll always have me."

Quentin bobs his head. "I'm sorry we'll miss your wedding," He holds up a hand. "Not that I expected an invite." He smirks. "I know Sam and I have invaded your personal life more than you've liked since you came back to Bennett Falls. I'm sure you'll be happy to see us go."

Being around Quentin and Samantha hasn't been easy. It's hard to pretend that the two people who used to be among my closest friends didn't stab me in the back. But it's also hard to pretend things didn't work out exactly how they were supposed to in the end. I'm marrying my best friend, and Quentin got the girl of his dreams. I'd say we both won.

"How about we just be happy for each other?" I say.

Quentin bobs his head. "I can do that."

The door to Cup of Jo opens, and Samantha walks in for the first time in a long time. She's been hiding from the public as much as possible since the baby was born. The second she sees us, she makes a B-line for the table.

"Did you tell her?" she asks Quentin.

"I just did."

Samantha throws her arms around my neck and cries on my shoulder. "Oh, Jo, I'm going to miss you so much."

I take a deep breath and meet Cam's gaze. "I'll miss you, too," I manage to say.

Quentin mouths, "Thank you" as he stands up. "Sam, sweetie, we should go. We have a lot of packing left to do, and Cam and Jo have to get back to work."

Samantha finally releases me. "I'll send you pictures

of Quentin Junior once he's home, and Christmas cards. I'll send Christmas cards. Oh, and of course you'll be invited to Quentin Jr.'s first birthday party and his baptism and—"

Quentin wraps his arm around Samantha and pulls her away from me. "Jo knows, Sam. She knows."

"You're the best friend I've ever had. Other than Quentin," she adds, smiling at him. I'm glad to see they've worked through the issues they were having. I suspected it was the pregnancy hormones making Samantha so angry with Quentin all the time. Couples counseling must have helped them see that.

"Take care of each other," I say.

Quentin extends his hand to Cam. "I won't tell you to take care of Jo because I know you will."

Cam bobs his head as he shakes Quentin's hand. "I wish all three of you a lot of happiness."

Samantha starts crying again.

"Come on, Sam. Let's go home." Quentin turns her toward the door, and Mo walks in as they leave. Quentin pauses and meets my gaze. "You'll always be one of the best people I'll ever know, Joanna Coffee."

After he walks away, Mo says, "Why does it sound like they're leaving for good?"

"Because they are," I say. "They're moving. They just came to say goodbye."

"Wow. What's Bennett Falls going to be like without Quentin and Samantha Perry?" Mo asks.

"I have no idea." I brush a single tear from my left

eye. Quentin and Sam have caused me so much grief over the years, but part of me is sad to see them go. That chapter of my life is coming to a close, and I have no clue what's in store for me next.

If you enjoyed the book, please consider leaving a review. And look for *Mocha and Manslaughter*, coming soon!

You can stay up-to-date on all of Kelly's releases by subscribing to her newsletter: http://bit.ly/2pvYT07

Cup of Jo

Coffee and Crime

Macchiatos and Murder

Cappuccinos and Corpses

Frappes and Fatalities

Lattes and Lynching

Glaces and Graves

Espresso and Evidence

Americanos and Assault

Doppios and Death

Ristretto and Revenge

Piper Ashwell Psychic P.I. Series

A Sight For Psychic Eyes

A Vision A Day Keeps the Killer Away

Read Between the Crimes

Drastic Crimes Call for Drastic Insights

You Can't Judge a Crime by its Aura

Fortune Favors the Felon

Murder is a Premonition Best Served Cold

It's Beginning to Look a Lot Like Murder

Good Visions Make Good Cases (Novella collection)

A Jailbird in the Vision Is Worth Two In The Prison

Great Crimes Read Alike

I Spy With My Psychic Eye Someone Dead

A Vision in Time Saves Nine

Never Smite the Psychic That Reads You

There's No Crime Like the Prescient

Fight Fire With Foresight

Something Old, Something New, Something Foretold, Corpse So Blue

Murder is in the Eye of the Beholder

Between a Vision and a Hard Case

There's More Than One Way to Sense a Killer

Madison Kramer Mystery Series

Manuscripts and Murder

Sequels and Serial Killers

Fiction and Felonies

Holidays Can Be Murder

Valentine Victim

Fourth of July Fatality

Traumatic Temp Agency

Corpse at the Candy Shop

Tragedy at the Toy Shop

Paranormal Books:

Touch of Death (Touch of Death #1)

Stalked by Death (Touch of Death #2)

Face of Death (Touch of Death #3)

The Monster Within (The Monster Within #1)

The Darkness Within (The Monster Within #2)

Unseen Evil (Unseen Evil #1)

Evil Unleashed (Unseen Evil #2)

Into the Fire (Into the Fire #1)

Out of the Ashes (Into the Fire #2)

Up in Flames (Into the Fire #3)

Dark Destiny

Fading Into the Shadows

The Day I Died

Replica

ACKNOWLEDGMENTS

As always, huge thanks to my editor, Patricia Bradley, for your amazing feedback on this book. My books are in such great hands with you. Ali Winters at Red Umbrella Graphic Designs, thank you for another completely amazing cover and for being so easy to work with.

To my family and friends, thank you for your continued support of my books. To my VIP reader group, Kelly's Cozy Corner, and my ARC team, thank you for reading and spreading the word about my books. I couldn't do this without you. And to you, my readers, thank you for making time for my books. I hope they bring you as much enjoyment as they bring me.

ABOUT THE AUTHOR

Kelly Hashway fully admits to being one of the most accident-prone people on the planet, but luckily, she gets to write about female sleuths who are much more coordinated than she is. Maybe it was growing up watching *Murder, She Wrote* that instilled a love of mystery, but she spends her days writing cozy mysteries. Kelly's also a sucker for first love, which is why she writes romance under the pen name Ashelyn Drake. When she's not writing, Kelly works as an editor and also as Mom, which she believes is a job title that deserves to be capitalized.